Abbie sho
of her as far a
and she fervently hoped that the two seats next to her would remain empty. She was in no mood for casual airplane chitchat. From her seat, she could see down the length of the plane, and it appeared most of the passengers had already boarded and seated themselves.

Good, she thought with satisfaction, stretching her legs in front of her and placing her paperback on the seat next to her. *What kind of idiot takes an 8 p.m. flight to Anchorage, Alaska, in September anyway?* She leaned her head back and closed her eyes. *Besides me.*

Abbie let loose a sigh which began deep within her soul. It came out louder than she planned, and she hoped no one on the quiet plane heard the understated groan. She opened her eyes and found a tall man standing in the aisle next to her seat. Startled, she blinked and met a pair of almond-shaped, obsidian eyes that crinkled at the corners. His friendly smile widened to a grin.

"May I?" he asked, indicating the window seat past her.

"Oh, sure." Abbie quickly scrambled out of her seat and stepped into the aisle to allow him to pass. She caught her breath when he slid past to take his seat. His face was strikingly handsome. Exotic eyes were the prominent feature in an angular bronze face with a narrow nose and full lips.

As the plane rolled onto the runway, Abbie leaned her head back and closed her eyes for a moment. It wasn't too late. She could still jump up and ask the attendants to stop the plane and let her off. She smiled imagining the scene. Would they open the doors and let her out onto the runway to trudge back to the terminal on foot? Would they take the airplane back to the terminal and boot her out the door—forbidden to book a flight with them again? A quiet hysterical giggle escaped her wayward lips. Or would they force her to inexorably march on and continue the flight to Anchorage against her will?

A Sigh of Love

by

Bess McBride

A Sigh of Love

Contact Information: info@thewildrosepress.com

Cover Art by *Angela Anderson*

The Wild Rose Press
PO Box 706
Adams Basin, NY 14410-0706
Visit us at www.thewildrosepress.com

Publishing History
First Champagne Rose Edition, 2007
PRINT ISBN 1-60154-177-5

Published in the United States of America

Dedication

As always, for Cinnamon

Chapter One

"Well, I'm going, Cassie." Abbie's voice quivered.

"Are you serious?" squeaked her best friend.

"Yes."

"I-I don't know what to say. I can't believe it. Don't get me wrong. I think it's a great idea. You don't know how long I've wished you..."

"I know, I know," Abbie murmured. She nervously rifled through the pages of an old *Smithsonian* magazine while she listened to her friend on the phone. Distracted by the face of a handsome Native American man for a second, she impatiently tossed the magazine aside and gripped the phone tighter.

"Call me if you need anything, sweetie. I wish I could be there for you. I think this is fabulous." Cassie had obviously warmed to the idea. "You have to follow your dreams, Abbie. This might be the one."

"I hope you're right, Cassie. I really hope you're right." Abbie paused, unwilling to let her confidante go. "I'm scared," she fussed.

"I know you are," Cassie soothed. "I know. Listen, everything's going to be great. I believe with all my heart that everything will go your way."

"Thanks. I'd better let you go. I know you've got a lot to do. I'll talk to you soon, okay?"

"I'll be out of touch for a while, so I'll call you when I can." Cassie's solicitous voice eased Abbie's anxiety.

"I'm going to miss you...especially now."

"I'll miss you too. I can't wait to hear how everything turns out. Bye, Abbie."

****

Abbie shoved her carry-on bag under the seat in front of her as far as it would go. At present, she had the row all to herself. In no mood for casual chit-chat, she fervently hoped the two seats next to her would remain empty. From her vantage point, she could see down the length of the plane, and it appeared as if most of the passengers had already boarded.

Good, she thought with satisfaction. She stretched her legs and placed her paperback on the seat next to her. *What kind of idiot takes an 8 p.m. flight to Anchorage, Alaska, in September anyway?* She leaned her head back and closed her eyes. *Besides me.*

Abbie drew her brows together and frowned as she settled in for the four hour flight to loneliness, emptiness, and stupidity. But, she reassured herself, it would only last for less than a week. Then she could return to her life in Seattle—of loneliness, emptiness, and stupidity.

Abbie let loose a sigh which began deep within her soul. It came out louder than she planned and she hoped no one else on the quiet plane heard the understated groan. She opened one eye to discover a tall man standing in the aisle next to her seat. Startled, she blinked and met a pair of almond-shaped, obsidian eyes that crinkled at the corners. His friendly smile widened to a grin.

"May I?" he asked, indicating the window seat past her.

"Oh, sure." Abbie quickly scrambled out of her seat and stepped into the aisle. She caught her breath when he slid past to take his seat.

His face was strikingly handsome. Exotic eyes were the prominent feature in an angular bronze face with a narrow nose and full lips. Those same lips continued to smile politely. With a quick nod of thanks in her direction, he shed his dark green jacket and sat down, laying it on the seat between them.

Abbie settled back into her seat and buckled the seatbelt. With a sideways peek at her seatmate, she forgot her earlier wish to be alone.

Mesmerized by the long black hair, which began in a distinctive widow's peak at his high forehead, she followed its length to the middle of his back. He wore it secured in a ponytail at the nape of his neck. She had a momentary tantalizing vision of his sleek black hair unbound, framing his high cheekbones. Abbie suspected Alaska Native heritage, though she'd never seen such a tall Native American.

He reached to pull a magazine from the seat pocket.

Abbie's bemused eyes followed every move of his long brown hands. When the magazine sat unopened in his lap, she raised her eyes to his face and found him watching her, watching him. Black eyes smiled.

Abbie dropped her gaze to her lap and nonchalantly picked up her book. She pretended to read, but found it difficult to focus on the book. The compelling presence of the stranger distracted her.

"Ladies and gentlemen, could I have your attention?" the flight attendant sang out from the front of the plane.

Abbie attempted to focus on the attendant's safety instructions, reminding herself that she might one day regret not knowing where the exits were. This could be that day, she thought with a faint smile.

The plane began to move backward and Abbie peered past the handsome man's shoulder to watch the airport recede into the distance. He turned and caught her eye. With a quick smile, she turned away to gaze out the window on the other side of the plane.

Great! He must think I can't take my eyes off him. She strained her neck to see out the other side. *Hey buddy, I'm just trying to look out the window. Get over yourself.*

Abbie's lips moved silently as she mouthed her thoughts. She pressed her lips tightly together to keep her self-talk in and her mouth shut, stealing another quick glance back at her seatmate. Abbie suspected he must be well used to women ogling him. He really had to be one of the most striking men she had ever seen. She admired the dark brown flannel shirt and well-fitting dark blue jeans that lent him an outdoorsy look and she wondered what he did for a living.

As the plane taxied down the runway, Abbie leaned her head back and closed her eyes for a moment. It wasn't too late. She could still jump up and ask the attendants to stop the plane and let her off. She smiled, imagining the scene. Would they open the doors and let her out onto the runway to trudge back to the terminal on foot? Would they take the airplane back to the terminal and boot her out the door—forbidden ever to book a flight with them again? She stifled a hysterical giggle. Or would they force her to inexorably march on and continue the flight to Anchorage against her will?

Abbie opened her eyes when she heard the roar of the engines. The plane raced down the runway. She peered out the window on her side of the plane as they lifted off the ground and straight into the dark eyes of the man who watched her.

"Hi, my name is Tom," he said in a deep timbre and reached out an inviting hand.

Surprised, but delighted by the unexpected resonance of his voice, Abbie returned his handshake.

"Abbie."

"Are you headed to Alaska or continuing on from there?"

"I'm going to Anchorage," Abbie replied, unsatisfied with her short answer, but unable to think of anything particularly witty to say. She certainly had no intention of telling anyone why she was on her way to Alaska.

"Me too," he said companionably.

Abbie returned his smile and let her gaze wander out the window. The lights of Seattle fell away, and the plane headed out over the water.

"Are you going to Anchorage for business or pleasure?" he pressed.

She brought her gaze back to his face. He seemed intent on being chatty. A friendly seatmate was the last thing she had wanted on this nearly empty flight, but that was before she knew a conversationalist could come in such a striking package. Out of the corner of her eye, she spied a good number of open seats. But at this point, she had no intention of moving away from the man whose hair she longed to touch.

She sighed wistfully as she prepared to answer without the slightest intention of giving him any real information.

"Just a visit," she said with a brief but polite smile. She found it hard to meet his direct gaze, afraid her eyes would reveal her attraction.

"I see," he said in that wonderfully deep voice. With a brief nod and a polite smile, he continued reading his magazine.

Abbie could have kicked herself for her standoffish reply. Tom could possibly be the only person she would have a conversation with for the next week. She certainly didn't want to return home and tell Cassie she'd spent an entire week in Alaska and talked to no one. She ransacked her brain for a friendly question.

"So, Tom, are you traveling to Anchorage for business or pleasure?" *Weak, Abbie, very weak.* It was, after all, the same question he'd asked her. But in her depressed state, her social skills lacked spontaneity.

He glanced up from his magazine, eyebrows raised in surprise, but replied, "I live there. I'm just returning from a conference in Seattle."

Abbie wondered if she dared ask the most pressing question on her mind. She plunged ahead, "Are you...? I mean...are you an Alaska Native?" She cringed in case she had guessed wrong. She knew some people did not like to be asked about their ethnic origin.

To Abbie's relief, Tom grinned.

"Not a bad guess. What gave it away? The long hair?" He grabbed his ponytail and shook it once before throwing it back over his shoulder.

Despite her sour mood, Abbie responded to his infectious smile.

"Yes, I'm half Athabascan on my mother's side. My dad is white. How about you? Where do you get your long hair?" he asked with an admiring glance at the thick corn-colored hair she also wore in a ponytail.

She blushed at the look in his eyes. "The length comes from my Scot-Irish genes I guess, but the color comes from whatever the latest bottle of hair dye fades it to, I'm afraid," Abbie said with a wry grin.

Tom laughed, and Abbie's pulse quickened at the sensual sound.

"I can't say I've ever heard that response before," he chuckled.

"Do you ask the question often?" she retorted, beginning to enjoy herself.

"No. Actually, I don't think I've ever asked a stranger about her hair before. You'd be the first," he said with telltale color staining his cheeks.

Utterly charmed to see him blush, Abbie guessed he didn't flirt much, which suited her fine since she was perfectly awful at the game. She broke out in a sweat every time a man tried to flirt with her, which probably accounted for the significant lack of romance in her life. She changed the subject to something less intimate.

"What kind of conference were you at?" she inquired politely, watching his high cheekbones return to their normal bronze hue.

"An anthropology seminar at the University of Washington. Very boring, I'm afraid."

Abbie found it hard to tear her eyes away from the warm smile that lit his face.

"Anthropology? Really?" she prompted with interest.

"Yup, anthropology. I'm a professor at the University of Alaska in Anchorage," he said as if it were the most mundane job in the world.

Abbie was impressed. A professor! Of anthropology, no less! Anthropology had been her favorite subject in college, but she couldn't pursue a degree in the field because she'd had small children. She couldn't have left them to go out on the two to six-week archeological digs required for the degree at the time. Abbie had changed her major and pursued a less adventurous degree in medical administration. She now worked for the government as a medical records administrator, a job that afforded her a satisfactory income, but little in the way of excitement.

"Well, that must be interesting," she added in an effort to continue the conversation.

"It used to be...when I was younger and could get out into the field. But I've been teaching for about 20 years now, and I think I'm about ready to retire." He turned away and gazed out the window with a furrowed brow.

Abbie studied his lean face and wondered what troubled him. It seemed obvious that something weighed on his mind. He had a decided slant to his dark eyes that gave them a faintly Asian appearance. His long, straight nose and strong chin lent his face a distinctly uncompromising look, but she remembered how his expression softened and his eyes warmed when he smiled.

"I can't believe I just said that. I don't think I even knew I felt that way." He shook his head slightly and grinned. "You aren't a therapist by chance, are you?"

Abbie chuckled. "No, nothing so glamorous, I'm afraid. I work in the records room of the VA Hospital in

Seattle as a medical records administrator. But I think I would rather have your job."

Tom grinned. "Well, you're welcome to it if you like. The students would probably appreciate someone new and different. I'm sure the faculty would. They must be quite tired of looking at my mug after all these years."

Abbie couldn't imagine anyone tiring of his handsome face, but she simply smiled in response. She didn't miss the note of affection in his voice when he mentioned his students and his colleagues, and she wondered again why he was considering retirement. He certainly looked young, though she guessed he must be in his mid forties if one calculated the length of time necessary to obtain a PhD in anthropology and subsequent twenty years of teaching. His hair showed no signs of graying. She sighed, unconsciously brushing a stray tendril of her own hair which had shown silver since her late twenties.

"Why the big sigh? That's the second one I've heard from you. You were sighing when I got here. I hated to disturb you to sit down because you seemed so...um...sad."

Startled, Abbie stiffened. He certainly was observant. She hadn't realized she'd done it again.

"Oh, don't worry about me," she laughed it off. "I always do that or so I've been told. I sigh when I'm sad or happy or glad or mad or discouraged." She smiled disarmingly. "Just now, I was pouting because I don't see an ounce of silver in your hair even though I'm guessing you might be in your forties." She pulled her own ponytail forward. "I started turning gray when I was in my twenties. Scot-Irish genes again, I guess."

"I'm forty-six. Good guess." He reached over to touch a lock of her golden hair. "Athabascan-German genes, I guess," he teased. "I do have some gray, though. Wait until you see it in the sunlight."

Abbie's eyes flew to his face. Touching her hair seemed like such an intimate thing for a stranger to do. Tom must have realized it at the same time because he pulled his hand back and gripped the armrest.

"Sorry," he chuckled as his face colored again.

"That's okay," Abbie responded, her own cheeks flushed from the unexpected contact.

Tom turned toward the window, while Abbie focused

on the attendant approaching with her cart. She welcomed the distraction.

"What can I get you?" asked the young blond woman with a bright smile.

"Do you have tomato juice?" Abbie asked.

"Yes, we do. And for you, sir?"

"I'll take a coffee, please," Tom replied.

Drinks were served and the attendant moved off.

Abbie glanced at her watch. Almost 9 p.m. Another three hours until the flight landed in Anchorage.

"I can never sleep on these flights, so I load myself with coffee to help me forget about being tired." Tom poured cream into his coffee.

"If I drank coffee, I'd be sipping gallons of it. I don't sleep well on planes either," she smiled. "I get a crick in my neck and then the whole trip is ruined."

"Why don't you drink coffee?" he asked casually.

"Oh, I gave it up long ago. It makes me cranky. So one week when I had a cold and couldn't taste anything, I quit drinking it. I'm pretty sure I developed the caffeine withdrawal headache, but since my head already hurt from the cold, it didn't seem to matter much. I didn't think I'd ever be able to give it up." She sipped her tomato juice and wondered if she were rambling, fairly sure her story sounded dull.

What are you babbling about, Abbie? Hush!

"Good for you. I'd love to give up coffee. I just don't seem to have the willpower. Perhaps you can give me a few tips." He raised an eyebrow and eyed her with interest.

Abbie dropped her eyes to her juice as an excuse to break the uncomfortable intimacy of the eye contact. She couldn't remember the last time a man had actually listened to something she had to say.

She realized with a start that his attention not only lifted her spirits, but made her temporarily forget her reason for coming to Alaska. When she deplaned though, and entered the empty airport, she would remember all too clearly why she'd made the fruitless journey.

"There's that sigh again," he said, with a curve of his lips and a dancing light in his eyes. "I never did find out why you're going to Anchorage. Most people who travel for pleasure usually do it in the summer. Don't get me wrong," he protested. "The weather is still good. The temperatures have been pretty comfortable in the low 60s, so you'll have a pleasant stay. But the tourist season is over for the most part." He raised his eyebrows questioningly.

Abbie didn't know what to say. She wasn't about to tell him the truth. At least, she hoped she wasn't. Though who knew what she might say once she started babbling.

"Umm...I used to live in Anchorage actually, and I'm just on my way back for a visit." Let him think what he would.

"Oh really? When did you live in Alaska?" he asked with apparent interest and shifted in his seat to face her.

Abbie's breath caught in her throat. She'd been satisfied with the restricted eye contact necessitated by their side to side positioning, but now his steady gaze held her eyes. She wanted to break the lock, to look away, but she couldn't—short of falling out of her seat. She backed up as much possible in the small, cramped space.

Tom's eyes followed her adjustment. He gave her a small reassuring smile, but did not break the intimate eye contact.

She stammered, "Oh...about ten years ago. We lived in Anchorage for about three years."

"We?"

"My children and I," Abbie reluctantly clarified. She didn't want him to know about her boring and dull life, though she didn't really understand why. He was just a stranger on a plane.

"How old are your children?"

Abbie rubbed her hands together nervously. "Kate is twenty and Tim is twenty-two. Tim works as a geologist in Hawaii and Kate is away at college."

"And your husband?" he asked with a flicker of dark lashes. His eyes traveled to her hands.

"No husband. Not for a long time," she clasped her fingers together tightly and fixed him with an over bright smile.

"Me too." He smiled sympathetically.

"No husband?" Abbie quipped to ease the tension. His revelation and the gentle understanding in his eyes caught her off guard.

Tom laughed, a deep-throated sound that thrilled her.

"No. No husband. No wife. I've been divorced for...oh...about twelve years now." He hesitated. "It's tough, isn't it?"

Abbie nodded mutely, but she didn't trust herself to continue the thread.

"Do you have children, Tom?"

"No, sadly, we never did." He offered no further explanation.

Abbie stared at her glass of juice, her mind busily searching for a less intimate topic. She came up empty.

"You said you used to live in Anchorage. What made you move down to the lower forty-eight?"

Abbie smiled at the Alaskan term for the forty-eight contiguous states. It had been ten long years since she had heard Alaskanisms such as this one. She realized she missed the language unique to Alaska.

"Do you know, I haven't heard that phrase since I left?" she grinned at him.

"The lower forty-eight?" He chuckled. "I know what you mean. When I use that expression in Seattle, no one seems to know what I'm talking about. I have to remember to leave the colloquialisms at home when I travel outside."

"See? There's another one. *Outside*. Outside of Alaska. You don't hear that everywhere." Abbie laughed, something she had not done in some time. The sense of joy invigorated her.

"I can't help myself," Tom joined her laughter. "It's an Alaskan thing."

"I'd forgotten." Abbie wiped her moist eyes and caught her breath. "I've been gone too long," she added, an unexpectedly wistful note creeping into her voice.

Tom pressed. "You never did answer. Why did you leave?"

Abbie hesitated. She wanted to tell this man the truth and couldn't understand why. She glanced up quickly to see the warm smile that gave his face an openness and vulnerability which belied the mysteriousness of his dark eyes. His attentiveness was intoxicating, something she had not experienced in years.

"I took the kids home to Seattle to live near my parents after my husband and I divorced. We'd only been in Alaska for three years and I thought my kids needed family. I felt so isolated up there. My ex-husband left Alaska and moved back East with his new girlfriend."

Abbie turned from his sympathetic gaze and stared down at her clasped hands. The topic never got any easier. Even after all the intervening years, she still felt ashamed, inadequate, and fairly sure the failure of the marriage had been her fault.

"They're married now and have two children." She glanced back at Tom quickly and gave him her best independent and liberated smile.

"I'm sorry," Tom said quietly. "That must have been rough on you and the kids."

Abbie's eyes traveled back to her hands. "Yes, it was, but it was a long time ago. I'm over it now," she finished brightly, hoping she appeared confident and serene.

"Well, good for you. I'm not sure how people ever get really over it. Infidelity, I mean." His voice deepened as he looked out of the window at the dark night outside.

Abbie waited with bated breath. Would he say more?

He turned back towards her. "My wife left me as well...for someone else."

Abbie's eyebrows shot up in surprise. How could anyone leave this gorgeous man?

"I'm sorry," she said hesitantly. "So, I guess you know I've been fibbing," she added with a rueful smile. "I'm *not* over it. I'm not sure I'll ever get over the betrayal."

"I figured that. Your face was a little too happy when you claimed to be...uh...*over it*."

His smile of camaraderie and understanding captivated her, and Abbie had the craziest desire to slide into the seat between them and lay her head on his shoulder. She wondered what it would be like to hear his deep voice rumble in her ear as she lay against his chest. She sighed.

"There you go again," Tom smiled gently. "A sigh."

Warmth stole into her cheeks. She avoided his intent gaze.

"So, did you tell me who you're visiting in Alaska?"

Abbie's face drooped. She had hoped to get through the entire week without explaining the reasons for her trip. Wasn't it enough simply to say she was visiting? Would other people press her for more details as Tom did? She realized that Tom's question was normal and not particularly personal, but she really did not want to explain. She planned to sightsee over the week and return home with pictures to send to her kids who had been ten and twelve years old when they left Alaska. The kids had kept up correspondence with childhood friends, though Abbie hadn't made any close friends in Alaska. She'd met some of the other parents, but work and motherhood had kept her far too busy for more intimate relationships. With her ex-husband's frequent absences as an airline pilot, she'd often felt like a single parent, and all of her free time had been consumed by the children and their activities. It seemed, however, that Steve had plenty of time for intimacy on his journeys, she thought for the thousandth time.

Distracted by bitter memories, she realized Tom still awaited her answer.

"I'm sorry," she shook her head to dispel thoughts of her ex-husband. "I'm just taking a trip back to Alaska to sightsee. I'm not really visiting anyone in particular." She found it hard to meet his gaze and felt inexplicably awkward lying to him. He was just a stranger, after all. Besides, she wasn't really lying. She wasn't visiting anyone. Not any more. Not since the phone call last week...

Chapter Two
The previous week

"Hi George, how are you?" Abbie forced a confident and breezy note to her voice when he answered the phone.

"Oh hi. I'm fine. How are you?" George responded in monotone.

She was nervous as usual when she called George at his home in Anchorage. She usually waited for him to call because she didn't want to seem pushy. But he hadn't called in over a week and she needed to talk to him immediately. With a rigid back, she perched on the edge of her desk chair.

"I'm good." The silence dragged as she waited for him to ask about her flight's arrival time. She'd been surprised when he hadn't called earlier to get her travel arrangements.

She hesitated. "George?"

"Yes?"

"Umm...I'm sorry about bothering you. I've been waiting for you to call."

"I've been busy at work."

Something's wrong. His voice. He lacked the usual enthusiasm she had come to expect on their hour-long phone conversations between Seattle and Alaska.

"George, is everything okay?"

"Sure."

"I booked my flight," she rushed on hoping against hope that his short answers reflected only a pensive mood.

"Really?"

Her stomach twisted. *This is not going well.*

"Do you want to know when I get in? Are you going to pick me up?" It had never occurred to her that he wouldn't. She had booked her arrival and departure times to coincide with his free time from work, assuming they would spend time together and she would not need a rental car.

The silence on the other end of the line grew to deafening proportions, but she forced herself to press ahead.

"George?" she asked in a small voice. "Is something wrong? Last week you asked me to call you when I booked my flight. You said you were going to pick me up at the airport."

"Listen, Abbie," he paused. "I don't think this is working out."

"What?" she gasped.

He'd been asking her to meet in person since they'd first been introduced by his cousin, Sara, a sweet coworker of Abbie's. Abbie and George had corresponded by phone for the past three months. She hadn't dated in years, and felt giddy, romantic, and young again as they discussed their lives, their grown children, future plans, and Alaska.

She knew deep down it was an unrealistic relationship. After all, they lived 3,000 miles apart. How were they going to see each other? Was she going to move to Alaska? It would be a crazy idea for her to pack up and relocate to a remote state where she didn't know anyone.

But Abbie was a romantic...or she was a fool, and now she was fairly certain it was the latter as she struggled to understand what George's words meant.

"I don't know what you mean. *This isn't working out.*" She struggled without success to keep her voice from quivering. What would she do with the nonrefundable tickets and a phone that didn't ring anymore?

"I mean we don't have anything in common. I don't even know you, and you don't know me. This phone thing...I don't think it's been going well. Do you?" He paused. "Maybe you should cancel the reservations."

To George's credit, he did not hang up right away. Abbie had no intention of telling him the tickets were nonrefundable. What was the point, she thought dejectedly? She doubted he would care anyway.

"I thought once we met, we might find more in common. It's so hard to get to know someone over the phone."

You're begging, Abbie. Stop it! You're making a fool of yourself.

"I agree. It *is* hard. Look, Abbie, I'm sorry, but I think this has been a mistake."

Abbie's face burned with shame. Her stomach twisted into knots. Dry lips stuck together, making it hard to speak. *He's going to hang up. Say something, Abbie, something profound, something that'll hurt him like he's hurt you!*

"Listen, I have to go. Take care. Goodbye." George rushed through his final impersonal words.

Abbie held the dead phone and stared at it. What had happened? Last week, he'd begged her to come for a visit, and this week, when she'd finally made the reservations, he changed his mind and ended their budding relationship.

A wave of humiliation washed over her. She knew Sara would feel awful about setting her up with such an unreliable and fickle man. Or maybe she'd secretly blame Abbie for George's rejection. She'd have to tell Sara tomorrow that George had changed his mind about meeting her. Sara knew Abbie had already bought the tickets, and she'd been enthusiastic about playing matchmaker for two of her favorite people. Abbie hated to disappoint her.

She felt foolish, inadequate, and generally unlovable. After all, she must have done something wrong to make George change his mind. Was it something she said? Maybe she'd been too willing to fly all the way to Alaska to visit him? Did she seem desperate? Too lonely? Maybe he thought if she couldn't find someone in a large city like Seattle, she must be too homely. She *had* sent him her photo at his request, and he'd seemed pleased with her appearance.

What was she going to do with roundtrip tickets to Alaska? Go by herself? And do what? Abbie tried to visualize a long, lonely week of mumbling to herself. Who was she going to talk to for a week? What if she went anyway and George called to say he'd changed his mind, that he'd made a mistake and he wanted her to visit him after all?

Abbie gave a short laugh. That seemed unlikely. She'd made a mistake—an embarrassing one—but other than Cassie, Sara, and her daughter, no one would ever know about her foolish romantic dream. Thankfully, she hadn't told her son about George. Tim had grown into a very logical young man, and he would never have understood her desire to run away to Alaska to find love and companionship.

She couldn't help but feel a small measure of relief. It *had* been flattering to have George call her weekly, but she wasn't sure they shared any common interests other than loneliness. She'd foolishly assumed and fervently hoped that George had inherited some of Sara's sweetness as well as her loyalty and sincerity. After all, they'd been raised in the same family, hadn't they? Although George's voice lacked Sara's warm tone, Abbie had been willing to meet him in person and give him half a chance.

Abbie continued to stare at the silent phone. George wasn't going to call back and tell her how sorry he was for his momentary aberration, was he? It was just as well, she sighed. She studied the travel itinerary she'd printed out from her computer. What was she going to do?

The answer seemed clear.

She would go to Alaska. Alone. She'd visit the old neighborhood, their house, the school. She would rent a car and travel around to see how things had changed since her family left. It would be okay, as long as she didn't have to tell anybody how she came to be there by herself.

****

The arrival of the flight attendant with their meal provided a welcome interruption from the depressing thoughts. By airline standards, the dinner was quite large—a sandwich, chips and a small slice of cake. Abbie eagerly dug in.

"You look hungry," Tom chuckled as he tackled his own food.

"I'm always hungry," Abbie smiled back at him. "I should have packed a few snacks in my carry-on."

"I was wondering. How will you be getting around Anchorage when you get there?" He neatly changed the subject. "I mean...I could give you a lift somewhere if you like. My jeep is at the airport."

The generous offer surprised her.

"I have a rental car reserved," she sputtered. "I hope

it's not snowing yet. I haven't driven in snow in a long time, and I'm not sure I want to immerse myself in an Alaskan winter at 11 p.m."

"I'm pretty sure there's no snow down in Anchorage yet. You've got time. The weather has actually been pretty pleasant. You should have a good visit." He chewed his food thoughtfully. "If I'm not mistaken, the state fair starts tomorrow. You're in luck. Did you ever go when you lived there?"

"Oh yes! My kids loved the fair. And the food! I loved the food, especially those great big bread bowls of clam chowder. I haven't had one of those since I left." She stopped short of licking her lips.

"I like the chili bowls. My parents used to take my sister and me to the fair every year when we were kids. It was much smaller then. The giant cabbage contest always fascinated me. They still hold it every year, and the cabbages keep getting bigger and bigger. The largest so far has been 105 pounds. Can you believe it?" He grinned. "What do you suppose they feed those things?"

Abbie found his youthful enthusiasm endearing and infectious. Her troubles melted away while she listened to him reminisce about various childhood trips to the fair.

The flight passed quickly as they exchanged stories of Alaska. All too soon, the attendant announced preparations to land. Anxiety and disappointment struggled for supremacy when Abbie realized the flight was near its end. Impending loneliness awaited her just around the corner.

She glanced at her watch. Time had flown by, an apt metaphor.

Well, even if I never get a chance to talk to another soul in Alaska, the chance to talk to Tom on the flight has been well worth it.

She imagined telling Cassie and Kate about him when she recapped the trip on her return.

Girls, he's the most handsome man I have ever seen. He's got this incredibly long, jet black hair and dark eyes to match. Full lips that...

Abbie paused with a sly grin. She would edit her description of some features depending on whether she was talking to her daughter or her best friend.

Full lips that...give way to a beautiful smile. Oh, and his personality. He is warm and humble. You'd never believe a man that striking could be so kind and approachable. But, he's too good looking for me. Way out of my league. Too much for one woman to handle.

She sighed.

"I guess we're about to land," Tom stared out the window into the darkness and then turned to her. "Abbie, I'm not sure what your plans are while you're here, but I'm going to take a chance. Would you like to go to the fair with me day after tomorrow?" He rushed to finish. "I know I'm a stranger, but I hope you'll consider it. I'm harmless. I don't bite." He gave her a tentative grin.

Abbie melted when she saw color rise to his cheeks. He seemed as nervous as she felt.

Should she go? It would be wonderful to spend a day in his company. She could just stare at him all day long and listen to the timbre of his seductive voice.

But Abbie feared her apparent lack of emotional control. She'd foolishly run all the way to Alaska in search of some mystical idea of romance, a silly idea in hindsight. She doubted her ability to remain detached around Tom. Her heart already skipped a beat...or two when he spoke in his melodious way and gazed at her with those gentle dark eyes.

She was obviously a basket case who couldn't control her emotions. All she needed to do was fall for one more guy who lived 3,000 miles away—who was probably taken anyway. She didn't even know if he was involved in a relationship. He'd been divorced a long time. Surely, there had been other women.

"Abbie?" he prompted. "Does your silence mean no?"

"No, I'm sorry. No. I was just thinking...you know...about my itinerary," she lied. She wanted to be with this stranger more than anything else, but her eagerness had gotten her into trouble before.

"Umm..." she hesitated.

In the absence of an answer, Tom spoke again.

"How about this? I'll give you my card. Call me tomorrow if you want to go the following day." He bent his head to peer into her downcast eyes. "You look like you're unsure and I don't mean to push you."

Abbie took his card and closed it in her fist. She fixed blurring eyes on her lap and fought for control, picturing the endless, lonely days ahead. Why didn't she jump at the chance for companionship?

Say yes, Abbie! Say yes!

She cleared her throat. "Thank you, Tom. I *will* call. I'm just not sure what my plans will be. I appreciate the offer. That was very nice of you."

"You're welcome, Abbie. It wasn't meant to be just a nice gesture." He gave her a quizzical look. "I look forward to going to the fair with you. I hope that you *do* call."

He turned toward the window once again. Abbie followed his gaze and saw the lights of Anchorage appear in the darkness. The well-lit city glittered against the black night like a chain of gold on a bed of dark velvet. The city spread out as far as she could see. She knew it was bordered by the Chugach Mountains to the east and the waters of Cook Inlet to the west, but she couldn't make them out. She looked forward to the sight of the snow-capped mountains and the calm waters of the inlet tomorrow when the sun came up.

Abbie studied Tom's profile as he watched the ground below. She wondered about his parents and how they came to be together given their different cultures. What was his childhood like? Why did he choose to teach anthropology? What would happen if she really did call him and he changed his mind or, worse yet, didn't remember who she was? What would it feel like to touch his striking face and run her hands through his silky hair?

She sighed.

****

Tom stared out the window of the airplane, but he wasn't focused on the night sky. He thought about Abbie. Although an enigma, she fascinated him. Maybe because she seemed to be withholding information. He still wasn't sure why she had really come to Alaska or why she traveled alone. He didn't buy her story. She didn't seem like a person who enjoyed being by herself. He'd met his fair share of loners here in Alaska, a refuge for many people who wanted to run away from the world. In fact, he considered himself a loner which is what surprised him most about his spontaneous invitation to the fair. It had been years since he'd gone. But the enthusiasm on her face and her obvious desire to go encouraged him. He clenched his jaw slightly at the sting of rejection. She'd gone from happily chatting about the fair to a cold and withdrawn excuse not to go with him.

He couldn't figure women out, and he didn't know why he found this one compelling. She didn't even live in Alaska. What was the point of thinking about her when she would only be here for a week? The last thing he needed was a pen pal who lived in another state. He'd once tried a long distance relationship with a woman he'd met at a conference, but his heart wasn't in it. It seemed like too much trouble, and she wouldn't to come to Alaska to visit. He visited her once, but they soon realized they had little in common outside of anthropology.

So why are you trying to make a date with this close-mouthed woman? She's doesn't even seem to be interested in you.

She looked past him out the window and he hesitated to turn around to meet her eyes. She *was* very attractive. Her beautiful corn-colored hair reminded him of the golden lights of the city below as did her amber eyes. They fascinated him with color changes from deep chocolate brown to liquid gold. He thought he'd seen tears in her eyes at one point.

I wonder what makes her so sad? Is she still in love with her ex-husband? She did say she wasn't over it.

He wanted to turn and bask in her bright smile, but he dared not while she stared out the window. Her smile seemed forced at times, but when she relaxed, its sunny flavor gave him a thrill of joy.

That's a great smile. Worth risking a rejection. I'm not ready to see the last of it.

He hoped she'd call. He regretted not asking her where she was staying, but it seemed likely she would tell him if she wanted him to know.

The plane's wheels touched down with a screech. And he sighed.

****

Abbie watched Tom walk out of the airport while she waited at the rental car counter. Few people milled about at this time of night, and the terminal seemed as empty and desolate as she felt.

Tom didn't see her waiting at the counter, and she had a final opportunity to study him unobserved. She doubted she had the courage to phone him. What she really longed to do was run to him, throw herself down at his feet, grab onto his long blue-jeaned legs, and beg him to take her along...tonight.

She swallowed hard and fought the neediness that consumed her. It seemed so desperate...so unhealthy. The reason she'd ended up alone at an airport in the first place.

Abbie gritted her teeth and stood her ground, willing Tom to walk out of her life. Feeling completely and utterly alone, she picked up the keys to her rental car and made her way to the car park and a small red sedan.

The quiet night air chilled her skin. The temperature in the car showed 45 degrees. On a positive note, Abbie was pleased to see that she had indeed beat the snow. It seemed unlikely that it would snow at lower elevations over the next week, and she was thankful she would have dry road conditions for the sightseeing she planned. Abbie left the airport parking lot and drove downtown to find her hotel. She'd picked one on a stretch of water called Ship Creek in downtown Anchorage. Familiar with the area, she looked forward to watching the local residents and tourists engage in combat fishing in the small river. For onlookers, it could be a hilarious event in which hundreds of people lined up along the bank to try to snag salmon as the embattled fish returned to their spawning grounds. For the fishermen, it was often a crowded, elbow-to-elbow, and frustrating exercise in catching the red fish that seemed determined to ignore shiny lures as they made their final journey upstream to spawn and die.

The hotel appeared clean and well kept. She took her keys from the sleepy desk clerk and dragged her small suitcase up to the room. The large, spacious room sported standard hotel furnishings. The king-sized bed appeared comfortable and quickly caught her tired eye. Abbie kicked off her shoes and sank onto it gratefully. Lying back, she wondered once again what she was doing in Alaska—alone. She should have come back years ago when her children were teenagers and able to accompany her. They would have enjoyed seeing the sights once again.

Abbie closed her eyes, and the image of Tom's face drifted into focus. What was she doing? Why hadn't she jumped at the chance to go to the fair with him?

Abbie rubbed her eyes and sat up. It was too soon. She didn't trust men, and she didn't want to be hurt by another one. Though she hadn't been particularly attached to George, she'd been humiliated and crushed when he rejected her after his come hither performance. What if Tom did the same thing?

Her eyes paused on the phone sitting on the nightstand. She looked down at her watch, 11:45 p.m. *Too late?*

She pulled Tom's card out of her jacket pocket and stared at it. The plain card provided his name, cell phone number, department at the university and his work number.

No, it's too late. I'll wait until morning.

Against her will and better judgment, she tossed good manners aside and picked up the phone.

Chapter Three

I'm such a fool. Calling a strange man at 11:45 at night! Who does that? Besides me?

She listened to the phone ring, desperately hoping he wasn't home and didn't have caller identification or an answering machine. What had possessed her to pick up the phone? She could have sworn her plan was to wait until morning to call him. She had no idea what she planned to say or even if she intended to accept his offer to go to the fair.

"Hello?"

Oh no, what am I going to do now?

"Hello?" he repeated. He sounded short of breath.

Abbie felt short of breath. Anxiety robbed her of oxygen. She plunged in. "Hello, Tom. It's Abbie. I'm sorry for calling so late."

"Abbie," he said in an elated tone. "You called."

Reassured, she continued. "Yes, I'm sorry for calling so late, but I was hoping you hadn't gone to bed yet."

"No, I haven't. In fact, I just got home. I have a bit of a drive to my house. Have you arrived at your hotel yet? Where are you staying? Do you mind my asking?"

Abbie loosened her white-knuckled grip on the telephone and relaxed to the sound of his deep, friendly voice. He seemed genuinely pleased to hear her voice, though she couldn't imagine why.

"No, I don't mind. I'm staying at the Cook Inlet Inn downtown. Have you heard of it?"

"Of course. This is a small town as you might remember," he chuckled. "Did you pick up your rental car? Did everything go smoothly?"

Touched by his questions, her heart melted at the concern in his voice. She sat up straighter and gritted her teeth, silently berating herself for acting like a marshmallow. *Get a backbone.*

"Yes, everything went well. Listen, Tom, I should let

you get settled in after your trip. I just called to accept your invitation to the fair. Is your offer still open?"

"I'm pretty well settled here in my easy chair. But yes, the offer is still open. I would love to take you to the fair. Day after tomorrow, right?"

Abbie imagined him sprawled out in an easy chair. She wondered if there was room in the chair for two. Good thing he couldn't read her mind, she thought with a blush. "Day after tomorrow."

"Good, it's a date," Tom replied firmly. "I'll pick you up at the hotel at 10 a.m. Plan on a long day. There's lots to see and do."

"Okay, Tom. Thanks."

"My pleasure. I'm not sure what your itinerary is, but I hope I see you before then. Remember, it's a small town. Good night, Abbie."

"Good night," Abbie said slowly, wondering how he would manage to see her before then.

She put the handset down and stared at it for a long time while she silently argued with herself. She wanted to spend time with him and a trip to the fair with a handsome man was a bonus on this otherwise hopeless trip. On the other hand, she didn't want to allow herself to develop a crush on him. She'd learned her lesson with George. No more foolish dreams of long-distance romances. She needed to ground her feet in a good dose of reality. In fact, she would probably be better off if she continued to avoid men altogether as she had since her husband's betrayal. Perhaps she was destined to live out her days alone in a rose-covered cottage with good books to read and two cats for company, while her children and yet unborn grandchildren stopped by on an occasional Sunday afternoon dinner.

Abbie sighed at the image of such an unfulfilling future. It appeared uncomplicated, but sounded lonely.

****

Abbie woke at 7 a.m. Light filtered in through a slit in the curtains, allowing her to see around the darkened room. She rose and opened the curtains to look out the window. She had a good view of the creek below. The tide was out, reducing the creek to a mere trickle of water. Later, when the tide returned, the creek would fill with rushing water, hardworking salmon, and hopeful fishermen.

She looked beyond to the opening of the creek where ribbons of water decorated the mud flats on Knik Arm, a stretch of ebbing and receding tidal water that ran north of Anchorage. The golden light of sunrise reflected in the small streamlets which were all that remained of the river at low tide. She remembered how full that body of water became as it rose between twenty-five and thirty feet when the tide returned.

The outline of snow-capped Mount Susitna lay visible in the distance on the other side of the waterway. The sight of the mountain nudged a faint memory of an old Alaskan Native legend that referred to it as the Sleeping Lady. The shape of the mountain resembled a sleeping woman and legend told the tale of a young bride who waited for her lover to return from war. Abbie couldn't remember the rest. Maybe Tom would know, she thought with a smile as she turned away from the window.

The blinking message light on her phone caught her eye and she wondered who could have called. Kate had her cell phone number as did Cassie. She picked up the phone and dialed the number for messages.

"Hi Abbie, it's me, Tom. I asked the hotel clerk to leave this message on your phone rather than wake you. Listen, I was wondering, would you like to have breakfast this morning? I may be a bit late in asking you. I'm not sure if you're going to get this message by the time you leave, but I'll keep my fingers crossed. Give me a call and let me know. You have my number."

Weak-kneed, Abbie dropped onto the edge of the bed. Breakfast! This morning? Why would he call and ask her to breakfast? Didn't he have things he wanted to do? Why would he want to spend time with a woman who was only visiting? Was he lonely? Surely he wasn't as desperate as she?

She recalled their conversation on the plane the evening before. He seemed intelligent, kind, amusing, warm-hearted, charismatic, and handsome—at a minimum!

No, he couldn't be desperate. Not the man she'd met. He probably had a girlfriend—or several—crawling all over him. His easygoing personality dictated that he would have lots of friends, associates from work, even family who would want to spend time with him. She knew she did!

So why would he want to have breakfast with a stranger, some odd woman he met on a plane from Seattle who was shy, monosyllabic, reticent, grouchy, depressed, and desperate?

Abbie's plans for the day had been hazy at best with no clear focus other than to wander around the city and visit her old home and the kids' schools. Eager to discover why he sought her out, she ignored the joyful beating of her heart and picked up his card. She read the number again and dialed.

"Hello."

She took a deep breath to steady her nerves. It failed to help.

"Hi Tom. It's Abbie."

"Good morning."

Abbie was sure she had never heard that particular greeting in such a sensual voice before. It seemed impossible, but his voice sounded huskier this morning than last night. She wasn't sure why she responded so acutely to its timbre, but she allowed herself to be swept away in romantic fantasies as he spoke.

"Good morning." She hoped he couldn't hear the breathless excitement in her voice.

"Can you make breakfast?" he came to the point.

"Yes, thank you. Where would you like to meet?" She pressed the phone tightly to her ear to hear every velvety nuance of his tone.

"I'll pick you up. How about the lobby? In an hour?"

"Sure." Her heart seemed to jump into her throat.

"I'll see you in a bit."

"Okay," she mumbled as she put the phone back in the receiver.

Abbie dropped back on the bed and wondered for the umpteenth time what she was doing. She tried a new approach—logical thinking. How long it would take to get over a broken heart? If she fell for him as she seemed likely to do, would her heart take twice as long to heal as it did to fall for him? Three times as long? It was a mathematical mystery—never her best subject.

How about a cold shower, Abbie? She shivered. *Okay, a hot one then. Anything to get your head out of the clouds.*

With a wry grin, she shook her head and climbed off the bed to head for the shower. Dropping her nightgown on the floor, she turned on the water and stepped into the hot steam in a daze. She shampooed her hair and scrubbed her head vigorously hoping to bring blood back into her brain cells, but nothing roused her from her dreamy stupor. She seemed inexorably destined to fall for a stranger and unable to exert the willpower to prevent it from happening.

****

Abbie watched Tom walk into the lobby, as striking in daylight as he had been last night. Glistening black hair and a clean shaven face hinted at a morning shower. Well-fitting blue jeans, a dark blue flannel shirt, hiking boots, and his green jacket completed the perfect Alaskan male ensemble.

He saw her at once and flashed a wide grin in her direction. She wondered again what sort of genetic mix had produced a man that attractive.

"Hello." He held out a hand to help her rise.

"Hi." Abbie shyly put her hand in his large warm grasp. The masculine feel of his skin sparked a warm sensation that spread throughout her body, and she pulled her hand out of his as soon as possible.

"Are you ready?"

"Sure," she replied and followed him out the door to a large jeep, not surprised to see he owned the epitome of a sport vehicle. He seemed very outdoorsy and she wondered about his hobbies.

"I'll take you to my favorite diner. I think you'll like it. At least I hope you will." With an easy smile in her direction, he pulled the jeep out of the parking lot.

"That sounds fine," she replied as she tried to pay attention to her surroundings. She continued to feel as if she were in a dream and hoped the fog would soon lift. What was she going to tell Cassie when she returned? That she remained in a perpetual daze the entire trip?

She tried to focus on normal day-to-day mundane conversation. "How did you sleep? You must not have had much rest."

"I don't sleep very long at night, unfortunately. I wish I could. It's been a problem for a while. How about you? Did you sleep well?"

"I think so. At least, I must have. I don't remember much about it."

"How does it feel to be back?" The jeep passed through the downtown area. Abbie studied the buildings with interest.

"Great, actually. I haven't had much time to soak it in, but I realize how much I've missed this place."

"Yeah, I know what you mean," Tom said with a sigh. "I've thought about leaving a few times myself. I even tried a stint in Hawaii and Wyoming, but I keep returning."

She looked over at him in surprise. She didn't think she could imagine him living anywhere but Alaska. Visions of Tom running along the beaches of Hawaii in a swimsuit with his hair flying in the wind made her smile. What a pin-up poster that would be!

"Hawaii, huh? Did you swim there?" she asked irrelevantly. "What were you doing there?"

He looked over at her with raised eyebrows.

"Did I swim there?" He laughed. "Yes, I swam there. Tried some surfing too, but that didn't take. I can pass for a Pacific Islander, but I've got snow and ice running in my veins, not tropical saltwater."

Abbie chuckled with him.

"I did some teaching at the University of Hawaii," he continued. "I really enjoyed it there, but my wife didn't so we returned to Alaska. Same with Wyoming, I'm afraid."

Abbie heard the regret in his voice. She could think of nothing to say, so remained silent. She was curious about his wife, but she didn't think she knew him well enough to ask about her.

He was silent for a few minutes as he negotiated his way through traffic and into the parking lot of a small log cabin diner sporting an Alaskan theme of miners and gold panning.

"I love eating breakfast here. They pile the plates full of food and you never leave hungry," he grinned as he held the door open for her. He led the way into the rustic restaurant.

"Well, hi, honey." A round redheaded woman of indeterminate age approached as they entered. "Welcome back. How was Seattle?"

"Good, Betty. You know, the usual. But look what I found." He chuckled as he pulled a reluctant Abbie forward. "Betty, this is Abbie. She's from Seattle. We met on the plane. She's visiting here for a while," Tom explained gazing gently at Abbie's flushed face.

"Hello." Abbie winced under the scrutiny of the waitress's sharp but kind blue eyes.

"Hello, dear. Well, any friend of Tom's is welcome here."

Betty grabbed a few menus and escorted them to a trestle table covered with a red and white checked cloth.

"Now, you keep your eyes on this fella, honey, cuz he is one of the sweetest and handsomest men in this town," Betty giggled as she beamed at the couple.

Abbie's eyebrows shot up and Tom's cheeks reddened.

"Oh Betty, stop, you're embarrassing her...and me."

"I've known him since he was a little boy coming in with his sister and his parents. By the way, your folks were in already this morning. They asked if I'd seen you yet."

Tom smiled at her as she poured coffee.

"I haven't called to let them know I'm back. Mom will probably give me a lecture," he ducked his head in pretend shame.

With a mock admonishing noise and a swish of her apron, Betty turned to wait on another table.

Tom seemed to sense Abbie's discomfort. "I'm sorry. I didn't bring you here to show you off or embarrass you. I really enjoy the food here, and I thought you would as well."

"Oh, that's okay. It's a nice place." Abbie avoided his empathetic gaze by looking around. She tried to relax, though she felt as if she sat on pins and needles. His parents had been here...in the restaurant. She had missed seeing them thankfully. She had no idea why Tom invited her to breakfast, but she was certain she did not belong in the bosom of his family. She was just passing through...as they say, a stranger in a strange land.

Feeling a sudden chill, she crossed her arms and met Tom's steady gaze.

"Are you uncomfortable here?" he asked quietly. "We can leave."

"Just a little bit, but it will pass," she responded, unable to lie to those penetrating dark eyes. "I'm fine."

"Good, I'm glad," he smiled. "I want you to be comfortable with me."

Abbie caught her breath and dropped her eyes to her menu.

"So, what's good to eat?" she asked in a lighter tone. She peeked at him from under her lashes.

Tom cocked his head in acknowledgement of the diversionary tactic and chuckled. She crinkled her eyes and responded in kind. He offered her a selection of some of his favorite meals. She picked one and they ordered when Betty returned.

The plentiful food tasted delicious as Tom predicted, and Abbie understood why he'd become a regular at the restaurant. It boasted a homey atmosphere where regular customers, casually dressed in jeans and flannel shirts, greeted each other and Betty as they came in for a leisurely Saturday morning breakfast and review of the day's news.

Abbie noted with amused affection that, although ten years had passed since she was last in Alaska, folks seemed much the same as when she had lived there. Snatches of conversation verified that the topics continued to range from the weather to local politics, fishing, and the latest bear sighting near town.

Her gaze returned to Tom's face. She blushed when she found him watching her.

"It doesn't change much around here, does it?" A slow, easy smile warmed his face.

"You must have been reading my mind," she laughed. "No, it doesn't. Everyone still talks about the same things. But I've missed it. Life seems a bit less complicated up here, you know. It's either hot or it's cold. The days are nineteen hours long or five hours short. Everything else seems to revolve around those basic facts. Does that make sense or am I just talking in circles?" she asked shyly.

"No, I know what you mean. I really do. Either the

salmon are running or the snowmobiles are running kind of thing, huh?"

"Exactly," she said triumphantly, pleased to find someone who understood her whimsical train of thought. "That's exactly what I mean."

Abbie put down her fork and wiped her mouth, satisfied by the big homemade breakfast. "Wow, that *was* delicious. I don't think I'll be able to eat for the rest of the day."

Tom hesitated. "So...what sorts of plans *do* you have for today? I know you said you have an itinerary and that you were visiting?"

Abbie squirmed in her seat, frantically wondering what to tell him. She'd been hoping he wouldn't ask specific questions about her plans, because she only had vague notions of aimlessly wandering around the city. It sounded hopelessly boring, and she wanted to present a more independent, adventurous spirit...whether it existed or not. She'd made tentative plans for the day after the fair to travel down the Seward Highway to revisit some of the sights along Turnagain Arm to see how the glaciers were holding up, and head further south to Seward, a small fishing village at the gateway to the Kenai Fjords, a majestic body of water and home to whales, seals, sea otters, and puffins.

But at present, the lull of good food prevented her from coming up with an inventive tale to dazzle him with her delightfully spontaneous nature...her alter ego.

"I really don't have any firm plans today. I was just going to revisit some old places in the city. You know, our old house, my kids' schools, and the downtown area. I thought I'd take some pictures for the kids." Her itinerary sounded flat and dull even to her. She stared unseeingly out the window at the busy parking lot and wished she had the energy to lie, to tell him she had fabulous plans to visit old friends and loved ones and would be very, very busy all day long.

"I've been thinking, but I hesitated to ask because I didn't know what you had lined up for today. I wondered if you'd like to spend the day with me."

She swung her eyes back to him, startled by his suggestion. Her first inclination was to run from what she wanted most. Had she sounded too lonely, too pathetic? Did he feel sorry for her? She swallowed hard. She hoped not.

"Wait, before you say no." He held a hand up as if to ward off a negative response. "I'd love to drive around with you and see where you used to live and where your kids went to school. I'd like to take you out to the university to show you where I work. We could make a great day of this. What do you say?" His enthusiasm was infectious.

She hesitated. What could he possibly have to gain by hanging around her all day? Wasn't there something else he'd rather be doing? Though thrilled with his suggestion, she worried she wouldn't be able to entertain him with vivacious anecdotes of her previous life in Alaska. She didn't actually have any to relate. Her entire Alaskan existence had revolved around the kid's activities in her husband's frequent absences.

"Are you sure you won't be bored? I don't know how exciting the day will be," she cautioned him.

"I don't need exciting, Abbie." Tom reached over to touch her hand lightly. "I'll be satisfied with just getting to know you better."

A shock ran up her arm at his touch and she trembled. Her eyes flew to his and Tom smiled in embarrassment as he removed his hand.

"Sorry," he said as he lowered his lashes. "That was a bit grabby."

"That's okay." She surprised herself by reaching over to brush his hand lightly with her fingertips, once again rewarded by the return of his grin and a daring look in his sparkling eyes.

Abbie blushed. "Okay, Tom, if you're sure you won't be bored. I'd love to have company for the day."

"Great. Are you ready to go?" he asked as he stood up.

To Abbie's dismay, he insisted on paying the bill.

"Well, Tom, thanks for bringing your lady friend in. I hope we see you again soon, sweetie," Betty said with a twinkle in her eye while she made change. She leaned toward Abbie to whisper conspiratorially. "He doesn't usually bring women in here. Not since..." Betty shook her head slightly. "Well, I don't see him with women very much. Hang on to him if you can, honey. He's a keeper." Betty winked and smiled broadly at Abbie, then turned back toward the register to give Tom his change.

"See ya, Betty." Tom opened the door for Abbie.

She wandered into the parking lot, taken aback at the forthright confidence shared by the waitress. Abbie studied the back of Tom's dark head as she followed him to the jeep.

Did Betty's comments mean he didn't date often? Or maybe he just didn't take women to breakfast. Maybe he cooked for them at his place.

Abbie avoided the thought, still unclear on whether Tom was involved a relationship at the present time. She hoped not—for both their sakes.

I'd be miserable if Tom had a girlfriend. I'm pretty sure his girlfriend wouldn't be very happy either. I'm not going to have anything to do with a man who's cheating—even if it is just a tour around town and a trip to the fair.

Tom opened the passenger door, and she climbed into the jeep. He hesitated at the open door for a moment.

"What was Betty whispering about? Do you mind my asking?"

Abbie hated to betray Betty, but she felt compelled to answer him honestly.

"She said you don't bring women in there very much and that you were a keeper." Abbie blurted out the words in embarrassment. Tom charmed her once again when color rose to his face.

"Oh, that Betty. She's matchmaking, I see." He seemed relieved as he closed her door and walked around to the other side of the vehicle.

"Were you worried?"

"Kind of," he admitted. "The last time I actually went in there with a woman was with my ex-wife, Debbie, a few years ago. Betty thought we were getting back together, but we weren't. I was hoping she didn't bring that up, but I wouldn't put it past her. She's pretty outspoken and chatty," he smiled ruefully.

"Yes, she seems to be," Abbie grinned. "And no, she didn't say anything about your ex-wife."

"Well," he rubbed his hands together. "Where shall

we go first? Do you have your camera with you?"

Abbie showed him the camera she had packed in her purse.

"Do you mind if we go to the Saturday market downtown? I know it's pretty touristy, and I'm sure it's much more crowded than it used to be, but I'd like to see it again." She was hesitant and unsure about what he was willing to see and do.

"Sure. I love the market. I actually like watching the tourists," he said conversationally as he pulled the jeep onto the road. "They're so darn eager to see everything. They bring a lot of money into the economy, so I'm not one to sneer at them. Besides, my mom owns a local travel agency, and she wouldn't let me get away with saying anything bad about her beloved tourists." He grinned as he looked over at her.

As they neared the downtown area, Abbie observed with joy that summertime Anchorage remained as festive as she remembered. Large luscious baskets of flowers hung from ornate lampposts along the streets and colorful blooms spilled over flowerboxes affixed to buildings and gracing the sidewalks. People flocked downtown to wander the streets and admire the lush growth of trees, grass and flowers made possible by the almost unending light of the long summer days.

The market seemed much larger and more crowded than Abbie remembered, but she happily wandered up and down the vendor rows with Tom while they discussed the various arts, crafts, and food for sale. She noticed with amusement that tourists occasionally paused to stare at Tom with his obvious Alaska Native heritage and distinctive long hair. He appeared oblivious to the stares and double-takes as he moved through the stalls. Other people of Alaska Native ancestry who sold artwork or browsed the stalls showed the same unconcern regarding the curious glances of visitors.

Abbie was taken aback when two older women with silver hair, white sunhats, and sporty leisure suits stopped Tom and asked if they could have their photo taken with him.

He gave them a huge grin and said, "Sure, ladies."

Abbie stifled a giggle when he put his arms around

the much shorter women and pulled them in close for the photo that a bystander was coerced into taking. The older women laughed in delight while gazing up at Tom with something akin to adoration on their faces. Abbie suspected she knew how they felt since it was all she could do to keep the same adoring look from appearing on her face.

Tom gave each woman a quick squeeze before he released them. He waved as they wandered off whispering to each other, giggling, and throwing longing glances back in his direction

"Well, Tom, you seem to be in your element. Does this sort of thing occur often?"

He winked at her. Her knees weakened at the gesture, and she wished she too could have been one of the women pressed up against him in an embrace.

"Happens all the time during tourist season," he chuckled. "It's the long hair," he said, tugging on his ponytail. "They get a kick out of posing with a local."

Abbie smiled and wondered if he had any idea how handsome he was. No matter what his ethnicity, she suspected the ladies would still have asked to have a picture taken with him because he presented such a striking figure.

"You don't think your looks have something to do with it?" she smiled brightly.

Color stole into his cheeks, giving him a boyish quality.

"Aw, come on. I look pretty ordinary around here. You should see my sister and my mother. Now, they're quite beautiful. Even Dad is a pretty good-looking fellow. I'm the runt of the litter," he laughed self-mockingly.

Abbie laughed at the ludicrous thought and shook her head with disbelief. He seemed genuine in his modest assessment of himself and his effect on people.

Tom grabbed her hand as the crowd grew thicker and urged her over to the food stalls to try some of the local foods. Although still full from breakfast, she looked forward to sampling some of the vendors' delights. They took their food to a nearby bench and sat down to eat while they gawked at the tourists who gazed back at them.

When they'd sampled as much food as possible, they left the market. Abbie directed Tom to the south side of the city where she planned to take photos of her old house.

As they approached the neighborhood, Abbie's pulse quickened and she broke out in a cold sweat. She cast a furtive look in Tom's direction, hoping he hadn't noticed her rising anxiety. She hadn't anticipated such a reaction to the distant memories of the house she and her ex-husband had shared. She breathed deeply through her nose, hoping Tom would not notice her heaving chest.

She directed him to the house, and he pulled up across the street from the beige two-story with green trim. A renewed sense of failure washed over her as she stared at it. Her plan had been to take a few photographs, but she found she couldn't move. The house seemed virtually unchanged...as perhaps was she.

The tree in the front yard had grown taller. Against her will, her wayward thoughts traveled back in time. A dark, bitterly cold Alaskan winter night when the kids had gone to bed and her husband told her he was leaving because he'd fallen in love with someone else. She'd sat at the kitchen table just inside the window now hung with lace curtains. She had cried for hours after he'd left the house with just one suitcase. She hadn't known what she was going to do or how she would tell the kids. Abbie hadn't even had the heart to cry out to her parents for help for two weeks after he'd left. When she finally called, they'd flown up to help her pack the furnishings and moved her and the kids back to Seattle while she readjusted to life as a single mother. Her readjustment had lasted for the past ten years, she thought ruefully. She still lived in the same condominium she'd bought with her share of the sale of the beige house.

Tom's warm hand covered hers as it lay on her lap. His touch comforted her, but it also weakened her defenses. She peered at him wordlessly and shook her head. Her eyes moistened, whether from grief or embarrassment about her silly reaction to the house, she did not know.

Stop this! Get hold of yourself. Just focus on the good times. We had lots of good memories!

She drew in a deep calming breath.

"I'm sorry," she said with a catch in her voice. "I don't know what happened. I would have never come back here if I thought I'd have such a strange reaction."

"It's okay," he said soothingly. "I understand."

She gave him a grateful nod and swallowed hard. With shaking hands, she stepped down from the jeep and struggled to focus her camera on the house. Several deep breaths later, she steadied the camera and took a few photos for her children.

Kate remembered little of Alaska since she had been so young when they left, and Abbie looked forward to bringing back some photos to help stimulate forgotten memories.

Satisfied she had enough pictures; she climbed back into the jeep with relief and directed Tom to the nearby elementary school. Abbie had many fond memories of the small school where her children had done their best to excel, and she experienced none of the grief that hit her when she first saw their old home.

"The kids loved this school. I remember dropping them off and picking them up, spelling bees and soccer, teacher's conferences, and band concerts. What a busy time in my life," Abbie laughed. "I can't believe I survived it." She shook her head in bemusement and glanced at Tom who studied the small school with interest.

"Somehow, I can't imagine you with grown children," he said with an appreciative gleam in his eye. "You don't look old enough to have kids in their twenties."

Now it was Abbie's turn to blush.

"Why thank you, kind sir. You flatter me," she said coyly.

Abbie jumped out and shot a few quick photos of the school from different angles. Satisfied with her self-proclaimed mission as family historian, she clambered back into the jeep, and Tom drove back onto the road.

"What other areas would you like to visit?"

"Are you getting bored yet?"

Well, of course he must be. He's really being so nice. Try to be more...entertaining, Abbie, more stimulating.

"Oh no, this has been very informative," he said with a thoughtful, lingering glance.

"Well, there are some lakes north of town where I used to take the kids fishing. In fact, I went fishing by myself a couple of times when they had other things to do." She continued to worry he would grow bored and mercilessly dump her off at her hotel.

Okay, maybe that's a bit of an exaggeration.

She hesitantly added, "I'd like to go back and see them. Do you mind?"

"Great. Let's go," he said with enthusiasm as he headed onto the main road. Within a half hour, they entered a wilderness area just to the north of the city where a small graded road led to various small lakes stocked with trout by the city for recreational fishing.

Several dusty minutes later, they arrived at the first lake, and Tom pulled the vehicle into an unpaved parking lot near the water's edge. Abbie stepped out of the passenger's side and walked around the jeep for an unimpeded view of the still water that perfectly mirrored the evergreen trees and the snow-capped Chugach Mountains in the distance. She beheld a spectacular sight, the likes of which she had not seen since she left Alaska.

She and Tom seemed to be alone at the small lake. Only the poignant call of the loons swimming among the marshes on the opposite shore broke the peaceful silence.

Tom came to stand next to her. They leaned against the side of the jeep in companionable silence and watched the abundant life teeming around the lake.

An occasional fish broke the surface to snap at an unwary insect. Beavers paddled toward a rounded stick-built house in the middle of the small lake.

Abbie finally heard the sound she didn't know she had been waiting for. She held her breath and scanned the trees and the sky above the lake.

"Do you hear that?" Abbie asked with excitement.

"Yes. Over there," Tom said pointing to the source of the screech, a bald eagle regally perched high atop a tree watching the fish...watching them.

"I haven't seen an eagle since I left here," Abbie sighed with sheer happiness. "This is so peaceful," she breathed.

Tom took her hand. Though the contact momentarily

startled her, she didn't pull away. She didn't want to. The warmth of his hand complemented and enhanced the serenity and beauty of the sight before them.

"Thank you for coming with me today, Tom. I've never actually been out here with an adult, and I'm grateful to share it with someone who can appreciate it."

"You're welcome." Tom gave her hand a quick squeeze. "I've never been to these little lakes on this side of town. They're really quite beautiful. I'm glad you brought me." He reached over with his free hand to brush a lock of corn-colored hair from her face, allowing his fingers to drift across her cheek. A tremor ran from his hand to hers.

Abbie's heart fluttered at the tender gesture. She couldn't remember the last time a man had touched her face so intimately. She averted her face, hoping her cheek did not reflect the heat where the seductive sensation of his touch lingered.

"Are there more lakes?" Tom asked in a husky voice, returning his gaze to the scenery.

Abbie took a deep breath and steadied herself.

"Yes, there are a few more lakes where I used to fish. Do you mind?"

"Not at all. I'm really enjoying seeing Alaska through your eyes. It's refreshing." He seemed to take a deep breath before he gave her a lopsided grin.

They got back into the jeep and continued down the road, pulling in at various lakes of different sizes and shapes, most of them quiet and devoid of people, although a few folks fished in canoes or cast out from the shorelines.

Tom and Abbie pulled over at a man-made fish ladder to watch exhausted sockeye salmon attempt to jump over the ladder and make their way into the lake on the other side of the road to their final spawning grounds.

"I wish I could just pick them up and help them over. They're so tired. It seems like such a sad journey, doesn't it? To make it out to sea and then return to their hatching place to spawn and die."

"I don't think I ever thought of it that way," Tom smiled. "They're fighters, that's for sure," he said watching the fish, bright red as they neared the end of their lives, trying to fly over the ladder.

"Is it still against the law to touch them?" Abbie asked sadly.

"Yes, I'm afraid it is. Something about impeding the natural movement of fish...even if it is with the best intentions."

She looked up at him with misty eyes.

"What a struggle they have," she said mournfully as she walked over to the lake on the other side of the road. Those bright red fish that had successfully made the jump milled about peacefully in the shallow waters.

"I'm glad we don't just die after we procreate. Our lives would be so short." She peeked at Tom with dancing eyes. "Mine would be much shorter than yours since I've already had my kids. You could still be spawning."

Abbie found herself laughing uproariously at her joke.

It wasn't that funny, Abbie!

She hoped she wasn't disintegrating into hysterics. Tears of laughter streamed from her eyes. She glanced at Tom to find him watching her with a strange light in his eyes.

Tom unexpectedly pulled her into his arms and bent his head to kiss her. Without thought, she instinctively wrapped her arms around his neck to pull his head even closer as she kissed him back. His embrace tightened, and she rose up on tiptoe to close any possible gap between them. His kiss was firm and insistent, and she lost herself in the magic of his lips. The world around her began to sway, but his strong arms kept her from falling to her knees.

He raised his head and loosened his grip around her waist as he looked down into her half-closed eyes.

"Wow!" He cleared his throat, but failed to rid his voice of its sensual huskiness. "I'm not sure what came over me. I can't believe I just did that. Are you okay?" he asked with a frown between his narrowed glittering eyes.

"Ummm...oh yes, I'm fine," she said backing away in embarrassment at her own loss of control. She avoided his intent gaze and turned to stare blindly out at the lake. "I'm sorry too. That's not like me."

"Hey." He tilted her head back with gentle fingers,

forcing her to meet his sparkling gaze. "I didn't say I was sorry. I just said I can't believe I did that." His color was high as he added, "I don't usually grab women and maul them. I hope I didn't scare you off."

Abbie's heart skipped at least one beat.

"No, I'm not scared. I didn't exactly run," she murmured. She closed her eyes against his seductive gaze.

"No, you didn't, did you?" He released her chin and put his hands in his pockets. "I'm glad," he said simply and turned to head back to the jeep.

Abbie followed at a slower pace wondering what had come over her. She touched her lips with her fingertips as she relived the passionate kiss.

Tom held the jeep door open for her and got in the driver's side after she was seated.

Abbie sighed heavily.

"You're sighing again," he said quietly. "I hope that's not a bad sign for me."

She managed to meet his eyes.

"Oh no, not at all. It's just a release of tension, I think."

"Well, I'm going to have to try that because I'm pretty tense right now," he said with a short laugh. Starting the vehicle, he moved out onto the road.

Her eyes flickered toward him uncertainly, and she wondered what the week ahead held for her.

Chapter Four

Abbie had calmed down by the time Tom pulled into a space in the empty parking lot of the University of Alaska. She didn't know what to think about their passionate embrace at the lake. Her thoughts ranged from chaotic to confused during the drive back into the city.

Neither she nor Tom had spoken since leaving the lake. Abbie cast an occasional sideways glance at him in an attempt to read his thoughts. His set face revealed nothing. Perhaps he didn't dwell on the kiss at all. Maybe it was a fairly ordinary event for him. He *was* a very friendly man. He probably had no trouble collecting women along the way. Kissing them could just be part of his normal approach.

Not so for Abbie. She hadn't actually kissed a man since her ex-husband. Not that she hadn't dreamed of falling in love again over the years that had passed since her divorce, but the demands of single parenthood with two busy teenagers left her with little free time. The worst moments had come late at night after the kids went to sleep, when she lay alone in her bed. The loneliness and sterility of her life were most acute in the darkness of her bedroom, and she had dreamed of a lover. She never saw his face...always a vague image, but she knew he would be kind, thoughtful, intelligent, and deeply in love with her.

Tom's kiss—and her desperation to return it—shook her understanding of herself. She'd always seen herself as a shy, reticent woman, not given to the *flames of passion* she read about in romance novels. Even so, she had believed her love life with her husband to be very satisfying. There had certainly been passion, but she'd never lost herself in magic like she had when Tom kissed her. In hindsight though, perhaps her husband had found her frigid. He *had* left her for a younger woman. She'd avoided men ever since, burying herself in the responsibilities of motherhood.

Abbie sighed as she watched Tom park the jeep. Her exhausted brain begged her to stop thinking. She gave in.

"We're here," Tom said in a chipper tone.

"It looks quiet." Abbie glanced around the parking lot.

"Saturday. Not too many classes on the weekends."

"Oh, of course."

Tom led the way into a nondescript brick building and up a set of stairs to the second floor.

"This is the Social Sciences Building." He led her down a wide hallway and pointed out various classrooms. The dark neutral carpeting and bland beige wall paint were unremarkable. Abbie scanned various bulletin boards laden with notices and flyers, but she couldn't stop to read them and still keep up with Tom's brisk stride.

"This is my office," he said, pushing open a door that led into a small room filled beyond its capacity with overflowing bookshelves. A small desk set in a corner seemed to droop under the weight of still more books and papers.

Abbie entered the room, her eyes round with awe. Tom followed her in, chuckling at her bemused face.

"Messy, isn't it?"

"Well, it's certainly...busy," Abbie's eyes continued scanning the chaos.

"I know. I keep meaning to clean it up. Some of those books on the shelves are very outdated. Sometimes, it seems like information in the field of anthropology hasn't changed in decades, and then there are times when new discoveries are made and we find we can't keep up with the findings and research stemming from those discoveries."

Tom shook his head with a rueful smile and cleaned off a chair for Abbie.

"Do you mind if I check messages on my phone? I've been out of town for a week."

"Not at all," Abbie replied and picked up a textbook on cultural anthropology from the floor beside her chair. She fanned through it casually and stole occasional glances at Tom.

The material in the book seemed familiar. She remembered her fascination with the study of different cultures. She'd taken the freshman college class as a lark, but had fallen in love with the mysteries of human culture and archaeology.

She heard Tom groan and glanced up to find a frown marring his attractive face. He set the phone down on the cradle with a crack and leaned back in his chair.

"Is everything okay?" she asked. Abbie had never actually seen him angry, but she had a good idea he was displeased now.

His eyes swept over her distractedly as if he'd forgotten her presence.

"I'm sorry. What did you say?"

"Is everything all right?" she repeated more timidly.

"Oh yeah, I'm just..." He stared at the phone on his desk with narrowed eyes. "I'm fine. Just a strange phone call, that's all."

Against her better judgment, Abbie pressed him.

"How do you mean?"

Tom glanced at her and back at the phone again as if it was a cobra. Abbie didn't think he would answer. When his eyes met hers once again, his expression changed to one of confusion.

"Well...I'm not sure why I'm telling you this. I doubt it would interest you." He hesitated. "My ex-wife called." He paused for an even longer moment and resumed staring at the phone. "She's in town for a few days and wants to have dinner with me. Tonight."

Abbie's heart sank. What concern was this of hers, she reasoned without success? She had only just met the man. Of course he had a past. He obviously had a present. And it was a certainty he had a future. But it would be without her, because she would be leaving Alaska in five days.

Abbie blinked rapidly as she tried to think of something mundane and appropriate to say. What she really wanted to do was throw herself in his lap, cling to him, beg him to forget his wife, and have dinner with her instead. What if he and his wife reconciled? What if they slept together tonight—after dinner? Abbie's throat tightened, and she wondered if she would see him tomorrow.

"Oh," was all she managed to say.

Tom dragged his eyes away from the phone and studied Abbie's face. She forced a pleasant smile and hoped her tension wasn't obvious.

"I'm sorry, Abbie. I was hoping you and I would have dinner together. I hadn't asked you yet, but—"

"Oh, that's fine. I had plans anyway," she babbled. "No need to apologize." Abbie's smile grew suspiciously bright, and she jumped up from her seat. It seemed like a fine time to leave.

"Abbie," he said softly as he stood and came around the desk. He bent his head and peered into her averted face.

"Abbie." Tom lifted her chin and placed a light kiss on the tip of her nose. "I'm sorry. Whatever it is she needs to discuss sounds serious."

Abbie closed her eyes briefly as she fought for control. He kissed her nose! The tingle on the tip of her nose lingered long after he lifted his head. She raised a hand to touch her face and then rapidly dropped it in embarrassment. Her heart melted at the sweet kiss.

"No, really, that's fine, Tom," she lied. "As I said, I already had plans for dinner."

"We're still on for tomorrow, right? I'll pick you up at ten?" he asked, leading them out of the building.

"Sure, 10 a.m. it is," she said gaily, though she continued to wonder if he would call her tomorrow and tell her that he'd be spending the day with his ex-wife. She steeled herself for the possibility and kept silent on the ride back to her hotel as did a seemingly distracted Tom.

"Goodbye," she said with finality, dragging herself out of the vehicle at the hotel entrance. She wished she'd taken a picture of him today in case she never saw him again. That possibility seemed more than likely.

"I'll see you tomorrow, Abbie. Have a good night." Tom smiled and waved as he pulled out of the parking lot.

Abbie walked slowly to her room and wondered what his ex-wife wanted. Did she come to town often? Were they still friends? Lovers? Was he still in love with his wife?

She entered her room and listlessly dropped onto the bed. The clock showed 5 p.m. The sun would not set for another four hours. She decided to shower, change clothes and hop into her little-used rental car to find a nice restaurant in town. There was no point in moping just because a man whom she met only yesterday couldn't go to dinner with her.

How silly is that! No point in wasting my time in Alaska pining for another man!

An hour later, Abbie drove her small rental car to one of Anchorage's finer restaurants on the recommendation of the hotel desk clerk. The clerk promised good food and a friendly atmosphere. Abbie's spirits lifted. She felt clean, refreshed, and ready to tackle the town on her own.

She pulled into the restaurant parking lot, climbed out of her car, and entered the rustic Alaskan log cabin restaurant. The dining room bustled with diners even at this early hour, but Abbie found herself promptly seated following an anxious moment with the hostess.

"How many in your party?" The hostess inquired politely, scanning the area behind Abbie.

"One," she mumbled.

"Just one?" the middle-aged, dark-haired woman asked in a volume guaranteed to turn heads in Abbie's direction.

"Yes, just one," Abbie reaffirmed her solitude. As she followed the hostess to her seat, she choked down self-consciousness at her solitary status. It was easier to pretend to be a high-powered executive in town for business. Her management persona *chose* to eat alone just to get away from the pressures of work. Though no one would know of her pretense, she felt better having created a reasonable story to explain dining alone.

Abbie sat in a secluded booth sporting red cushioned benches with high carved wooden backs. Wall sconces shed soft lighting along the dining room walls. She had plenty of privacy, though she wasn't sure that she wouldn't rather have been watching other people than staring at the empty booth across the aisle from her.

She took a quick opportunity to salute the absent George with her water glass and wish him an empty tank of gas on a dark road. And she continued to pretend she was happy as a clam. She dared not think about Tom. Not if she wanted to keep her smile plastered on her face.

As the hotel desk clerk promised, the food tasted delicious. The young woman waiting on her seemed friendly and kind. Abbie thought she saw a solicitous query in the young waitperson's eyes, but she stuck to her private pretense—so many colleagues, so little time. And she sighed.

Having lingered as long as humanly possible over her meal, she paid her bill and considered plans for the rest of the evening. She opted to return to the hotel and stroll down to the creek to see if anyone was fishing, though she hadn't paid attention to the tide tables since she had arrived.

She slid out of the booth and glanced toward the entrance. She broke out in a cold sweat when she saw Tom waiting for a table. He had changed clothes and wore a long-sleeved light brown pullover sweater with tan slacks. The lightweight sweater fit snugly enough to display a muscular chest and broad shoulders.

Abbie couldn't miss the beautiful dark-haired woman standing next to him. Her stomach twisted when she saw Tom's hand under the woman's elbow.

That looks pretty affectionate. Now I know how he feels about his ex-wife. She's gorgeous!

Before Abbie ducked back into her booth, she got a quick impression of a small, slight woman with long hair as dark as Tom's that shone under the restaurant lights. Almond-shaped eyes, so similar to his, marked her as an Alaska Native.

Abbie slid toward the wall and averted her face. The layout of the restaurant dictated they would pass by her table on the way to be seated. She cringed, hoping they would not see her so she could sneak out the front door without incident. She wondered in disbelief how she could possibly have been directed to the same restaurant Tom would choose to bring his wife

All too soon, she heard Tom's melodic voice as he and his ex-wife followed the hostess past Abbie's booth. From the corner of her eye, Abbie saw the small beauty throw back her head to laugh at something Tom said. His broad smile portrayed his good spirits. As soon as they moved out of her line of sight, Abbie jumped out of the booth and headed for the door. She made a dash for her car and flung herself in the driver's seat in a huff.

She was sure Tom hadn't seen her. What would he have thought? That she followed him? Well, how could she have followed him if she was there first? Hah! she thought victoriously. Take that!

Her short-lived defiance evaporated within seconds, and she morosely drove out of the parking lot to head back to the hotel. She arrived to find the creek at low tide, empty save for a few solitary ribbons of water. No fishermen lined the creek bank that evening.

I can't even find a few fish to watch. I guess it's TV for me on my first night in romantic Alaska.

Abbie headed back to her room and sank onto the bed. She drew the curtains against the still well-lit sky. She considered turning on the TV when she noticed the blinking message light on her phone.

Who would have called her? Her friends and family had her cell phone number. It couldn't have been Tom. She knew where he was tonight. It seemed obvious he would be busy all evening, she thought sourly.

She picked up the phone and dialed the message number.

"Hi, Abbie. It's Tom. It's just about 6 p.m. Listen, my ex-wife made other plans tonight saying that she hadn't heard from me in time, so I decided to take my sister up on a dinner invitation. I would love for you to come to dinner and meet her. You'd like her. I hope you get this message in time. If not, I'll see you tomorrow. I'm sorry I missed you."

His sister! Abbie could have smacked herself. She had spent the better part of the last hour moaning and groaning over the obvious affection between Tom and his ex-wife only to find out it was his sister.

Overjoyed with relief, she kicked off her shoes and danced around the room. "His sister, his sister," she sang.

Abbie listened to the message again and realized Tom had called at 6 p.m. when she was in the shower. How she wished she had not missed his call! Abbie swallowed hard. She wasn't sure she wanted to meet his family. What would they think of her? She wasn't an

Alaska Native...but then, neither was his father. Did it matter?

She fell down on the bed winded from her giddy dance.

What am I doing? What am I even thinking? I'm off on one of my romantic tangents again.

Abbie decided she needed a good dose of reality. She called her daughter, Kate.

"Hello?"

"Hi, honey, it's me," said Abbie.

"Hi mom. How's the trip going?"

"Well, that's why I was calling. Ummm...listen. I met a man."

"What? What do you mean you met a man? Did that guy, George, change his mind and decide to meet you after all?"

"No, not George. I met a man on the airplane. He's really nice. His name is Tom."

"Really?"

Abbie winced at the skepticism in her daughter's voice.

"Well, I just thought I'd tell you." She couldn't for the life of her remember why she'd called Kate in the first place.

"And?" Kate wasn't making it easy.

"He's nice, that's all. We spent the day together, and I think we're going to the fair tomorrow."

"Really?" Kate hesitated. "Well, that sounds nice, Mom. What do you hope to get out of this?"

There it was, Abbie thought. The dose of reality she'd been looking for from her level-headed daughter.

"I don't know. Companionship?" she tried feebly.

"I know you, Mom. You don't know how to say goodbye. You get so attached to people. Remember the exchange student from Australia who stayed with us for two weeks? You cried and cried when she left. In fact, you guys still exchange Christmas cards, don't you?" She laughed affectionately. "And what about when Grandma and Grandpa bought that condominium and moved to Florida last year? Admit it. You cried when they left too, didn't you?" Kate paused. She continued on a gentle but persistent note. "Are you planning on being pen pals with this guy? Fly up there twice a year to see him? You know, I wondered what you planned to do with George, but I didn't want to burst your bubble."

Her practical Kate. Just what she needed.

"I don't know, Kate."

"This sounds serious, Mom. I can hear it in your voice."

"Oh, I'm okay. It's just a little thing on a trip, you know?"

"I doubt it," said pragmatic Kate.

"Well, what if...what if someday...I decided to move...back to Alaska? What would you say about that?"

"Mom! Are you serious? You just met this guy."

Abbie swallowed hard at the incredulity in her daughter's voice.

"I know, I know. I'm not talking about him...exactly," she lied to herself. "What if I just wanted to move back here? What would you guys say?"

She could hear Kate thinking.

"Well...I don't know about Tim. He's in Hawaii after all. Why would he care? He's never in Washington. I'd be okay if that's what you want to do, Mom. I'm busy here in school, and you know Derek and I are getting married when I graduate next summer. I think he's planning on heading off to Portland for graduate school. So, we wouldn't be here anyway. You'll really be on your own down here next year."

Abbie knew all too well how empty Seattle would be with her parents and children gone. She'd been dreading the end of the life she'd known, boring and staid though it had been.

"Well, honey, it was just a wild idea. I don't have any plans to move up here. I thought I would always stay there in Washington, but with everyone gone, it seems kind of empty."

"Yeah, I know what you mean," Kate said sympathetically.

"Well, hon, I'm going to get ready for bed. I'll talk to you again in a few days, okay?"

"Okay, Mom. Have a good time. And don't get married without telling me first," Kate chuckled as she hung up the phone.

Abbie leaned back against her pillows and thought about the conversation. Kate had asked the questions Abbie needed to hear.

The shrill ringing of the phone startled Abbie out of her thoughts. *Could it be Tom?*

She grabbed the phone with a shaking hand.

"Abbie? It's me, George."

Chapter Five

Abbie jerked the receiver away from her ear and stared at it in stunned silence. *George!*

"Abbie? Are you there?" He chuckled nervously. "I'm sure you're surprised to hear from me. *Abbie?*"

She put the phone back to her ear. "Yes, I'm here. Hello, George."

"There you are. Hi, how are you?"

Abbie noticed his voice sounded different than it had in the past. Could it be because they had a better phone connection? Or was it simply that *she* was now in the same state?

Why is he calling?

"I'm fine, thank you"

"Well, I'm glad I was able to catch you. I guess you're wondering why I'm calling," he said tentatively.

That's an understatement!

She said nothing, but listened to the pounding of her heart against the receiver. She hoped he did not hear it as well.

"You're not saying anything. Are you still there?"

"Yes, I'm here, George."

"Oh good. Well," he paused, "Sara called me yesterday and said you were still coming up to Alaska. She told me where you were staying and that you had bought nonrefundable tickets, so you decided to come up anyway."

Abbie gripped the phone tighter.

Sara! Didn't I ask you not to let George know I was going to come anyway?

George continued. "She's pretty mad at me, thinks I treated you unfairly."

He paused, but Abbie couldn't think of a civil response.

"I'm sorry, Abbie. I feel bad about that last phone call. I wanted to call you after that, but I didn't know what to say."

Abbie held onto her grudge and had no intention of giving him the satisfaction of accepting his apology.

"Abbie? Are you talking to me?"

"I'm listening," she said without encouragement.

"I said I was sorry," he repeated in a gruff voice.

His vague apology failed to explain anything about his odd behavior.

"Sure, I accept your apology," Abbie said politely and insincerely.

"Good," he said quietly. "Can we meet?"

"Meet? I...I don't know," she stammered, her martyr's confidence shaken by his request.

Now he wants to meet? Is he serious?

"I'd like to make it up to you," he said in a sincere tone. "Could we have dinner tomorrow night?"

Abbie thought about Tom and the fair. He'd said they would be out until late. She didn't really know Tom. What if his ex-wife wanted to have dinner with him tomorrow night?

"I...I don't know. I think I have plans," she murmured.

"Plans? But I thought you came to see me. You said you didn't know anybody up here. How can you have plans already?"

Abbie pulled the phone from her ear and stared at it again. George didn't have any right to question her. What nerve!

Did she plan to tell him she had met someone? Not likely. What if she never saw Tom again after tomorrow? Should she just tell George to take a hike? The rest of the week stretched endlessly as she saw herself wandering the streets of Anchorage sniffing flowers, sampling food, gazing at tourists, alone...no Tom, no George.

She put the offending phone back to her ear. "Well, I'm sorry, George, but I *did* make plans. Would you like to meet in the morning for coffee? Here at the hotel?"

"Coffee, huh?" He paused. "Okay," he said grudgingly. "I guess we'll take it from there. I'll see you at 8 a.m., okay?"

"Fine, see you in the morning," she added her cheeriest note, but it fell flat.

Abbie hung up and leaned back against her pillows once again. What a busy night it had been. It seemed she had more companionship on the phone in her hotel room than she did on the streets of Anchorage.

Perhaps she ought to hole up in the room until it was time to leave, she thought ruefully.

Abbie undressed and prepared for bed. As she brushed her teeth, she wondered why she had agreed to meet with George. Though she had enjoyed their phone conversations to a certain extent, she knew they hadn't exactly meshed in interests and tastes. But she'd been so hopeful of a possible relationship that she had turned a blind eye—or ear—to their dissimilarities.

She reminded herself that her original reason for coming up here was to see him—because he had asked her to. She supposed she ought to at least see it through, now that he was willing, to discover if any sparks ignited between them.

Muttering to herself, she got into bed.

"I don't know if this is a good idea, Abbie. Something is definitely wrong."

She felt a bit queasy about meeting him. He had betrayed her trust—even before they had actually met—and she didn't know if she could ever forget that.

Abbie picked up her paperback hoping to immerse herself in the simplicity of the novel and forget about the confusion of her life at the moment. At least in a novel, one could peek at the ending and decide whether one wanted to follow through and read the book. Real life held no such guarantees, she thought with a sigh.

Not necessarily surprised to hear the loud ring of the phone once again, she looked at the clock. 9:30 p.m. It was still fairly early. Through a slit in the curtains, she could see that the sun was just setting.

"Hello?"

"Hi, Abbie."

"Tom," she exclaimed with pleasure. A thrill run from her toes to the top of her head. "I'm afraid I didn't get your message until too late."

"I was afraid of that. I'm sorry too. I would have loved for you to meet my sister. I'm sorry about the late invitation. It must have seemed rude."

"No, not at all."

Abbie hesitated.

"You're not going to believe it, but...I actually saw you at the restaurant."

"You were there?" he jumped in before she could explain. "Why didn't you say something? I didn't see you."

"I was just finishing as you and your...ah...sister came in."

"But why didn't you say anything to me?"

Abbie couldn't deny the persistence in his voice, though she hated to admit the truth.

What can I say?

"I...I thought you were with your...ex-wife, and I didn't want to disturb you," she stammered.

"Oh...I see."

"Yes," she said relieved that he accepted her explanation.

"Were you jealous?" he asked point blank.

Abbie gasped and clutched the phone tighter.

"What?" she stalled.

"Were you jealous?" he asked again, refusing to let her save face.

"Well, no...I certainly was not. Whatever gave you that idea? I...well, no. I have no right to be jealous. Are you kidding? No, I wasn't jealous. What you do in your life is your business. No," she sputtered and fumed.

She thought she heard a low chuckle through the receiver.

"Well, I would have been jealous if I'd seen you with another man."

His deep, husky voice sent ripples of delightful shivers throughout her body.

Abbie laughed, hoping the conversation would take a less intimate note. Her heart pounded, and she wondered how long it could keep up its rapid pace before it jumped out of her chest.

"Well, I hope you had a good dinner," she changed the subject in a vague attempt to divert him from the heady flirtation. She couldn't think straight.

"Yes, it was enjoyable. I haven't seen my sister in a month, even though we live in the same town."

"Oh."

"Yes, we're both pretty busy. Well listen, I just called to say that I was sorry to miss you at dinner. How about breakfast in the morning before we go to the fair?"

Abbie's hands broke into a sweat. She didn't want Tom to know about George, though she wasn't sure why. It wasn't like she owed anyone anything, she told herself. Besides, Tom's ex-wife was still in the picture, wasn't she?

"I can't," she murmured.

"Oh?"

"I'm sorry, Tom. I-I've got other plans."

"I see."

"I'll see you at ten as we planned, okay?" she asked tentatively.

"I'll see you tomorrow."

Tom's final words seemed a bit subdued, and she fretted as she hung up the phone. What had she done? Should she be meeting with George? Why did she feel guilty? She didn't know either one of these men.

She turned out her light and lay wide awake in bed as birds sang outside her window, oblivious to the darkening sky. Her thoughts were in turmoil, and she willed herself to put them aside by counting sheep. When she did finally drift off to sleep, she dreamt of riding a moose named Tom and swimming with a beaver who called himself George.

****

Abbie woke early the next morning. The sun already brightened the horizon. Perhaps it had never really gone down, she thought sleepily as she rose from bed. She crossed over to the window and gazed out at the creek.

A few fishermen lined the banks of the swollen creek, casting out lethargic lines in dwindling hopes of a bite. The creek now ran too high for good fishing, and the surge of salmon that came in with the tide no doubt swam low in the water determinedly ignoring fishing lures.

Abbie wondered if Tom fished. The subject had never really come up. Did George?

She left the window and padded across the carpeted floor to her luggage where she rummaged for something to wear. It would be time to meet George all too soon. While dressing, she prepped herself for her meeting with him. Having avoided any thought of him over the past few weeks in a futile attempt to forget about her humiliation, she couldn't remember details about his life.

Sara's cousin had come north to Alaska five years ago. He had an ex-wife and two children living in...Abbie frowned in concentration...New Mexico? She couldn't remember. He found work on the North Slope where he lived for up to three weeks at a time, returning to town during his week off. Abbie had booked her flight to coincide with the time he would be in down from the slope.

He seemed less than enthusiastic about his job, but said it paid the bills. He stated the irregular schedule prevented him from meeting any women locally, and he was grateful Sara had introduced them.

George once sent her a picture of himself sitting on a rock wearing blue jeans and a white T-shirt. His hair was thick and curly—a dark auburn similar to Sara's that Abbie had always admired. In the picture, he sported a mustache and a short beard. He hadn't been smiling, though Abbie wasn't sure if she could tell because of the facial hair. Unfortunately, he'd also worn sunglasses, so she could tell little about his eyes. She didn't know their color, shape, or whether they appeared honest and kind.

In short, his photo left her wondering what he really looked like, and she wondered if she would recognize him in the hotel restaurant.

She wracked her brain to remember any other details about him. Their conversations had consisted primarily of him discussing his job, his love of the Alaskan wilderness, old cars, motorcycles, and music. Abbie knew she at least shared his love of Alaska, but she wasn't sure what else they had in common. Loneliness? Wasn't that enough to bring two people together?

She ran a brush through her long golden hair and put on some light makeup. She'd decided on a pair of dark blue jeans and a long-sleeved red blouse she'd bought for the trip.

A harried glance at the clock revealed it was time to go downstairs. Her heart began to race. Why had she agreed to meet George? How was this lonely trip to Alaska suddenly becoming filled with so many people and so much anxiety?

She entered the lobby and spied him immediately sitting in a chair staring at the small flames in the rock fireplace. Though still early in the year for the fire, the hotel must have thought guests would enjoy the ambience.

She approached him with a pounding heart. He turned his head, saw her, and stood up.

She blinked rapidly as she looked up into a pair of bright blue eyes ringed with dark lashes. George was tall, and he gazed down at her with a reluctant white smile beneath his dark reddish-brown mustache. He still wore the short beard which gave him that rugged Alaskan look local men were often famous for. His hair was as thick and wavy as his photo, and he ran a hand through it as it curled just below his ears. She quickly took in the well-worn blue jeans, green T-shirt, and hiking boots.

Abbie held out her hand, and he enveloped hers with a large grasp.

"Abbie. Welcome to Alaska."

"Thank you," she replied as she withdrew her cold and shaking hand. "Are you hungry? Ready for breakfast?" she asked with a valiant attempt at confidence.

"Sure." He followed her toward the dining room. "I've never eaten here. Never even been in this hotel before," he said looking around with interest.

Abbie smiled at him as pleasantly as she could. Why had he asked her to come to Alaska and then rejected her? Would she find out today?

A young waitress seated them and brought coffee and menus.

Abbie studied him over the top of her menu trying to understand his character by the shape of his thick dark brows or the set of his uncompromising chin. A useless exercise, of course, but she couldn't help but try to interpret his personality through his facial features.

Abbie ate very little of her meal, much too tense to enjoy the food that settled heavily in her knotted stomach.

She watched George eat heartily, apparently oblivious to her lack of appetite or, for that matter, any awkwardness at all.

During the meal, he asked how Sara was doing and

discussed Anchorage, Alaska in general, and life on the North Slope. Abbie listened to him talk and realized she had forgotten one of his favorite hobbies. Talking about himself! She wasn't sure what he actually knew about her as she couldn't remember that he'd asked her very many details of her life.

The waitress refilled their coffee as George finished his meal.

Abbie looked down at her steaming mug and asked the question ever present in her mind.

"Why?" She met his eyes as steadily as she could.

"Why what?" he asked.

She took a deep breath. Surely he knew what she asked?

"Why did you repeatedly ask me to come up here and then when I made reservations, tell me it wasn't working out?"

George's eyes flickered away from her face.

"I don't know," he shrugged his shoulders and pushed his empty plate away. "I can't explain it. I don't know what to say."

Abbie stared, willing him to give her an answer.

He toyed with his coffee mug on the table.

"I hoped we wouldn't have to talk about this any more," he said with a frown as he glanced at her and then again at his mug. "I'm here now, aren't I?"

"Yes, you are." Anger welled up within her. He wouldn't even try. "But I think it's a little too late," she said with an air of finality.

He frowned. "What do you mean...too late? Then why did you come? Why did you agree to meet me this morning?"

Abbie felt better already. She was finally in control.

"As you already found out from Sara, I came up because I'd already purchased the tickets. Remember, I used to live here. I plan on visiting some of the old sights. I agreed to meet you because it seemed like the polite thing to do," she gave him a pointed look. "And I was curious about you—what you looked like in person, why you did what you did. I guess I hoped to get some answers."

To her surprise, George reached over to grab her

hand as it rested on her mug. She tried to pull away, but couldn't. His grip was strong.

"Listen, I said I was sorry. Now that you're here, I want to give this a try. Let's go up to your room and talk about it in private," he said firmly holding her hand in his roughened one.

Go up to her room? Was he serious? She had a bad taste in her mouth.

"What do you mean...go up to my room? We're fine right here," she said finally freeing her hand.

"Suit yourself," he shrugged his shoulders again. "I just think that's the best way to see if we're compatible. Just get right down to it."

Abbie's stomach lurched as she understood what he suggested.

"You know, George, you're about as crude as the oil you work with. Do you seriously think I would sleep with you five minutes after meeting you? After the way you treated me? You haven't even explained why you played this cat and mouse game with me."

George shook his head impatiently.

"I don't know why. I got nervous, I guess." He concentrated on his mug. "I thought it would be a great idea for you to come up here, but when you said you were actually coming, I panicked. It seemed too real. I didn't know what you wanted from me," he finished turning his palms up in a helpless gesture.

Abbie's anger drained away. She had to admit he did look nervous. She supposed if she had flirted with a long distance relationship, and he had come to town with high hopes—as she had to admit she'd had—she might have panicked as well. She stared at her coffee.

No, she thought. She would at least have been polite.

She sighed. "I understand what you're saying," she said with a small smile. "I might have done the same thing. It's one thing to imagine getting together with someone on the phone and quite another when the person actually shows up on your doorstep."

George pulled his hunched shoulders back and sat up straighter.

"That's exactly right," he said with relief. "So," he rushed, "can we try again?"

Abbie shook her head slightly.

"I can't, George. I just can't. I think there's too much water under the bridge," she said regretfully, hoping she wasn't hurting his feelings as hers had been hurt.

"You're up here for, what, five more days? Think about it." He glanced at his watch. "I've got to get going right now. I've got to meet someone. You said you're busy tonight," he gave her a curious look. "What about tomorrow? Do you have plans? I could show you around a bit."

Abbie hesitated. What was the point? Still, he was a handsome man and Sara's cousin. He might be better than being alone. Surely someone as good looking as George had a heart that was just as attractive? Somewhere...deep down?

"I don't know what my plans are. Can you call me tomorrow?" she asked as she stalled for time.

"Sure." He frowned, rose to leave, and laid money on the table for the check. He gave her a puzzled look and said, "I'll talk to you tomorrow then." Without waiting for her answer, he strode out of the restaurant.

****

Abbie wandered back to her room reflecting on the past hour. Had George really suggested they go to bed together to find out if they were compatible? He seemed a bit graceless, and she wondered how much experience he had with women. She didn't know any women who would have jumped at the chance to sleep with a man who had humiliated them. George actually seemed unaware of how hurt she had been when he rejected her. Was he that naïve? Or that cold hearted? Abbie shook her head.

Men, she sighed. She would never understand them.

****

Tom hopped out of the jeep and looked up at the sky as he strode into the hotel. The day promised to be beautiful. The sun shone brightly, the temperature was just about perfect, and the birds in the surrounding trees sang.

Birds singing! Get a grip, man! Get your head out of the clouds.

"Good morning." He approached the lobby counter for a newspaper to read with breakfast.

"Good morning to you, sir." A young blond girl who appeared to be just out of her teens handed him a newspaper in exchange for the money he proffered.

"It's a beautiful day, isn't it?" He nodded thanks and grinned.

"Uh...yes, it is." She stared at him and then blinked, delicate color flooding her cheeks.

"Well, thanks. I hope you get a chance to get outside to enjoy the day. The fair is going on, you know." Another wide grin.

"Oh...uh...well, yes, I know. We're hoping to go tomorrow."

Shy girl. Her face is bright red.

"Good, glad to hear it. Thanks again."

Tom sauntered off in the direction of the restaurant. He stepped through the open double doors to stand by the hostess podium. The sight of Abbie in a booth with a dark-haired bearded man immediately caught his eyes. Her back was to the entrance, but he could see that she held the man's hand.

Tom's eyes narrowed and he gritted his teeth, a surge of unexpected jealousy flowed through his veins. He backed out the restaurant quickly and made his way out of the hotel, ignoring the hotel clerk's wistful farewell.

Tom threw himself in the jeep and put his keys into the ignition. He paused as common sense urged him to slow down for a moment. He did not want to take off into traffic in his present state of mind.

Tom let his keys dangle in the ignition while he gripped the steering wheel with tense hands. He urged himself not to read anything into the sight of Abbie with the dark-haired stranger. He had no idea what was going on. And frankly, it wasn't really any of his business. He'd only known her for a few days. She was certainly free to do what she wanted.

Tom took a deep breath and reached for the newspaper with the intention of waiting in the jeep until 10 a.m. when he was to meet Abbie.

He stiffened. If they were still meeting. What if they shared some previous history? She had lived here before. And she wasn't telling Tom the complete truth at any rate. What if she cancelled their plans for the day?

Tom cursed himself for not checking the phone when he ran out of the house this morning, eager to start what promised to be an exciting day...with Abbie. Unable to sleep, perhaps due to anticipation, he'd arisen early, showered and decided on breakfast in the hotel where Abbie stayed.

Out of the corner of his eye, Tom saw the bearded man walk out of the hotel, get in an old truck, and drive away. He took another deep, steadying breath.

He wondered what to do. Go in and wait? Call Abbie and reconfirm?

Suddenly unsure of himself and disturbed by the violence of long-forgotten feelings of jealousy, he stepped out of the jeep and returned to the hotel.

"Welcome back," the hotel desk clerk sang with a bright smile.

Tom raised a preoccupied hand in greeting and tentatively stepped toward the restaurant. He stuck his head in the door and stepped in. Abbie had left. The hostess seated him.

Having lost his appetite, he ordered coffee and spread the newspaper out before him. He stared at the words, but read nothing.

He hated his feelings of jealousy. He'd sworn he would never again go through the pain and anger of loving someone who didn't love him...as he had with his faithless ex-wife.

Tom remembered teasing Abbie on the phone last night about jealousy if he saw her with another man, but it was only meant in the spirit of flirting. Now twelve hours later, when put to the test, it seemed he subconsciously spoke the truth.

He told himself he should back off a bit. Abbie could see whomever she wanted. He had no claims on her.

Images and sensations of their passionate kiss rose unbidden to his mind, and he shifted in his seat and reached for his coffee.

Testosterone Tom. He'd better get hold of himself or the day would be long. He smiled. Forget backing off. Maybe he needed to kick it up a notch.

****

Abbie glanced over at Tom as he drove out of town

and headed to the highway that would take them to the fair almost an hour away. She breathed deeply, hoping he wouldn't notice. He smelled clean and fresh as if he just showered. His face was clean shaven, and his black hair gleamed in the sunlight. Abbie chose to wear her own hair down today, but she brought along a clasp in case it got in her way.

She admired his well-fitting blue jeans and the dark green plaid long-sleeved shirt he wore with the sleeves casually rolled up to reveal strong arms. Abbie studied his warm brown hands as he casually draped them over the wheel. They were slender but sturdy and bore the signs of some sort of physical labor. Small dark scars of varying shapes and sizes marked his hands, though none looked recent. She wondered if he'd done construction or some other heavy work when he was younger.

"How did you sleep?" Tom glanced at her from under his lashes. The warm smile on his face gave his question an intimate flavor, as if he'd just rolled over in bed in the morning to face her.

A delicious warmth stole over Abbie's body at the image. *This is going to be a long day.*

"Fine, thanks. How about you?" she said casually, shyly avoiding any hint of intimacy.

"Okay. Lonely though." His eyes focused on the road though he wore a half smile.

Abbie caught her breath. His flirtatious response seemed out of character for the nice, polite guy she thought she'd met, but after his impulsive burning kiss the day before, she realized that Tom was a highly sensual man, given to passions which boiled just below the surface. She suspected he normally kept a tight rein on himself—usually.

She didn't dare respond and turned her attention back to the passing scenery to bring her wayward thoughts under control.

She sighed.

"Sighing again?"

"Was I?" she asked in a bemused tone.

"Hopefully, it wasn't something I said...again, was it?" he teased.

"Maybe it was," Abbie said, daring to match his

banter.

"Good," he said firmly turning his attention back to the road.

"Yes, good," she agreed, a small smile curing her lips as she pretended to stare at the road.

****

Tom took Abbie's hand and led the way into the fairgrounds.

His grasp was firm. His touch felt natural and very welcome.

The fairgrounds already bustled with people, even at 11 o'clock in the morning. Tom and Abbie wandered up and down the aisles, stopping occasionally at the booths to examine the items for sale. Abbie thought she recognized some of the same vendors who had been at the Saturday market the day before.

Though neither Abbie nor Tom was hungry, they decided to share a funnel cake to start off the day.

"We've got a lot to eat today, so let's get started early," Tom laughed as he put a piece of funnel cake into Abbie's mouth.

Abbie did her best to keep the powdered sugar from settling on her face, but she must have failed.

"You've got some sugar on the corner of your mouth," Tom said as he reached over with a gentle thumb and brushed it away. His hand lingered on the side of her face, and she looked up into his warm dark eyes. People strolled past them as they stood on the walkway in front of the funnel cake vendor, but she saw only Tom. Hearing her silent plea, he bent down and kissed the side of her mouth gently, and she welcomed the softness of his lips.

"I just had to kiss that sweet spot," he said in a husky voice as he straightened up.

Abbie opened her eyes slowly and gazed up into his sparkling eyes. With a quick grin, she took another piece of funnel cake and ran it across her lips before she popped it into her mouth. She looked up at Tom mischievously and wondered if he would accept her invitation. Her daring behavior surprised even her, but she felt safe.

Tom chuckled as he bent his head again to kiss her sweet lips lightly.

"Thanks. I think you're going to make *me* start

sighing in a minute. What's going to happen when we get to the barbecued ribs?" he asked with a wide grin.

"Maybe we should take the ribs to go," she blushed and chuckled.

Tom's brows shot up. His dark eyes glittered as he ran a sensual finger down her throat to the pounding pulse at the base. He swallowed hard, let out a deep breath, and bent to speak softly into her ear. "This is going to be a long day, isn't it?"

Chills ran up and down Abbie's spine at the delicious warmth near her ear.

He raised his head and laughed shakily.

"Let's start walking before we get ourselves into trouble," he said with a sheepish grin. He took her hand in his and resumed walking. Abbie remained intensely aware of his body next to hers, his strong and secure grip, and the memory of his voice in her ear.

They entered the exhibit where Alaska's famed giant vegetables were on display. Theoretically, the vegetables grew to fantastic proportions because of the extended sunlight during the nineteen-hour summer days of south-central Alaska. They would grow even larger further north where the sun never really set in the summer. Abbie and Tom walked along the displays, marveling at the enormous zucchini, some as large as a small dachshund. She pulled Tom over to look at a 35-pound cauliflower. Tom's beloved cabbage, the center of attraction, was 85 pounds this year.

"What do they feed these things? Do you think they take them home after the fair and eat them?" Abbie wondered aloud.

"I don't know. I never asked," Tom chuckled as they studied the monstrously large produce, some bearing award ribbons of blue, red, and purple.

He slipped his arm around her waist, and Abbie shyly leaned back against him. She wanted nothing more than to close her eyes and stand there for hours, but all too soon he took her hand and led her out of the building.

Abbie blinked as they stepped back out into the bright sunlight, immediately struck by the beauty of the mountains as they provided a stunning backdrop for the fairgrounds. Even at the end of summer, streaks of ice and snow ran down the crevices of the tall peaks. She sighed.

"A sigh?" Tom teased once again.

"Oh, I was just thinking how beautiful it is here in Alaska. I've missed it, and I've missed coming to the fair," she finished with a quick grin.

"I was hoping you'd enjoy it. Maybe it will be enough to lure you back to Alaska," he grinned and led her off toward the carnival rides.

Abbie snuck a startled peek at him as they walked along.

Lure you back to Alaska? What did he mean? Her heart gave a mighty thump as she considered the comment. He probably didn't mean anything serious by it, and he probably had no idea how anxious she was for a change in her life. Would he be part of the deal if she moved back?

Abbie gave her head a quick shake. She needed to stop thinking like that—like some desperate woman ready to fall in love with a complete stranger and run away to the wilderness, even though the idea held a certain attraction. Stop hanging onto his every word and expression, looking for some special significance.

She wished she could talk to Cassie, but she was already in Europe with her new husband. Maybe they had returned by now, Abbie thought wistfully. Cassie had told Abbie the incredibly romantic story of how she and her husband had fallen in love on a whirlwind tour of Europe, and she had encouraged Abbie to throw caution to the wind and go to Alaska to meet George to see if he was the man for her.

Abbie couldn't wait to hear her friend's reaction as she told her about George and Tom, and her confusion. She knew Cassie would understand. Abbie made herself a promise to call Cassie that evening when she returned to her room.

Abbie and Tom rode several carnival rides and ate more food as the day passed. They bought tickets to an outdoor concert and relaxed on the hillside enjoying the band. Tom stretched out on the grass apparently unconcerned by any possible green stains to his clothing. Abbie laid out her jacket and sat down on it beside him with her arms hugging her bent knees. She would have liked nothing better than to stretch out in Tom's arms and lie beside him, but she quickly squashed any such bold urges.

He laid his hand casually on her thigh as he watched the band on stage, and Abbie lost focus on anything other than the warmth of his touch. She stared unseeingly in the direction of the stage as she relished the sensations that ran through her body. At times, she felt warm all over, and then she would shiver with delight. Her thigh tingled, and her heart skipped the occasional beat.

"Are you cold?" he asked solicitously.

Abbie looked down at him, appreciatively taking in his strong jaw and full lips, his long hair lying on the grass.

"No."

"I thought I felt you shiver," he pressed with concern.

"I did," Abbie gave in. "But it wasn't from cold."

Tom looked up at her inquiringly. She blushed and looked back at the stage after she stole a quick glance at his hand touching her thigh.

"Oh," he said with a chuckle. "Do you mind?" he asked nodding in the direction of his hand.

"No," she replied. She longed to reach over and touch his face, his hair, his legs, anything, but she held back.

"This *is* going to be a long day," she sighed and forced herself to look away from his decidedly sensual body.

"Yeah, that's what I said," he sighed.

Their eyes met in shared understanding of heightened attraction, and they laughed.

Abbie's nerves were taut by the end of the concert. Her body tingled with desire, and she took deep breaths to try to calm down. As they left the outdoor theater, they parted ways to head to respective restrooms.

Abbie rinsed her face in cold water in lieu of a shower. She studied her reddened cheeks in the mirror and wondered what the rest of the evening had to offer. She didn't know if she wanted Tom to make love to her or not. Well, of course, she wanted him to make love to her, but she hadn't been with a man in such a long time that she was unsure of herself and afraid of the unknown. Would she be a good lover? Had she *ever* been a good lover? After all, her husband *had* left her for someone else. Maybe she'd been horrible in bed—inadequate, cold, lifeless. She hadn't thought so at the time. She'd naively believed that their love life was passionate and fulfilling. But it must not have been, she thought.

Abbie sighed. She'd asked herself these questions a million times in the ten years since the divorce, but she'd never found any satisfactory answers. With every year that passed, she'd thought about her marriage less and less, and she'd almost stopped wondering why Steve had left her. *Almost.*

Being with Tom and feeling the reawakening of passion brought the past sharply to the forefront, and she couldn't help but wonder. *Would she be a good lover?*

She gave herself a quick shake, patted more cold water on her face and neck, dried off, and decided the night would bring what it would. She would wait and see.

She stepped outside and walked right into George.

Chapter Six

"Abbie. What are you doing here?" George asked in surprise, grabbing both of her shoulders to steady her as she faltered.

"George! Uh...hello," Abbie stammered, searching for Tom. She didn't see him immediately and hoped she could get rid of George before Tom came back.

George wore the same clothing from earlier that morning. Abbie looked past him, but he appeared to be alone.

"So, what are you doing here? I would have brought you if I'd known you wanted to come to the fair."

"Oh, umm...I just decided to come. Are you here with someone?"

George's blue eyes narrowed at her vague response. To Abbie's relief, he finally dropped his hands from her shoulders.

"Yeah, I'm here with a buddy of mine. He's in the john."

"Oh...," Abbie's mind worked furiously trying to figure out how to give him the slip and find Tom, but she came up empty.

"So," he looked down at her with a skeptical expression. "You just decided to come out here today...at the last minute? It's odd that you didn't mention it at breakfast."

"Uh...no...I mean, well, yeah. We used to come to the fair every year when I lived up here." Abbie felt like she had been caught by her father with her hand in the cookie jar. "So here I am," she finished brightly.

"Here you are," George echoed. "Well, would you like to join us?"

"Oh, that's nice, thanks, but I can't." Abbie's eyes darted around. She finally located Tom standing a short distance away. He leaned against a wall, his hands shoved deep in his pockets, watching them with an unreadable expression on his face.

Abbie swallowed hard.

"I came with someone, and he's waiting for me. I'd better get going." Abbie glanced quickly up at George to see his brows draw together in a frown. His mustache and beard hid the rest of his expression.

"I see," he said. "The plans you had for today." He looked around. "You don't seem to be telling me everything. I thought you didn't know anyone up here anymore. Isn't that what you told me on the phone?"

Abbie's desperation grew as Tom continued to watch them.

George's eyes followed hers.

"Is that him?" he asked brusquely.

Abbie nodded.

"I'm sorry. I have to go, George," she said quietly as she turned to walk away.

George reached out to grab her arm. Her eyes darted to Tom before she looked back at George. She saw Tom straighten and start in their direction.

"I'll call you tomorrow. Just like we planned," George said harshly. He released her arm, turned, and disappeared into the crowd.

"Who was he?" Tom asked when he reached her side. "I was waiting for you to finish your conversation, but I got a little worried when I saw him grab your arm."

"How long have you been standing there?" Abbie avoided his question.

"I've been waiting for you to come out of the bathroom."

Tom looked down at Abbie with a frown.

"Do you want to tell me who he was? I saw you at breakfast with him, by the way."

Startled, Abbie looked up into his set face.

"I got to the hotel early to have some breakfast, but I saw you with him, so I decided to wait out in the jeep."

Abbie couldn't read his expression, but he wasn't smiling anymore.

"Oh," she filled in the dead space.

Tom continued to watch her. She noticed he did not take her hand, and she missed his warmth.

"You're not going to tell me who he is, are you?"

Abbie knew she had to tell him something.

"He's the cousin of a friend," she said simply, hoping Tom would take it at face value.

"I didn't know you were meeting anyone up here. I just got the impression you were on your own. I must have been mistaken," Tom said slowly with a shake of his head.

"I'm *not* meeting anyone. I mean, I wasn't...." Abbie felt like she'd sunken deeper into the quicksand. Couldn't the clock just turn back twenty minutes to when they sat on the grass next to each other and relished their mutual sensual awareness?

Tom waited for her to finish. Abbie didn't know what to say.

He sighed heavily.

"Well, listen. What do you say we wrap this day up? I've got a long day tomorrow, and I'd better make it an early night," Tom said in a flat voice. He glanced at her one last time before he moved away in the direction of the fairgrounds exit.

Abbie followed behind, hot tears burning her eyes. He didn't turn around, and he didn't take her hand.

He drove back to town in silence, his eyes fixed on the road ahead. Abbie wracked her brain for something to say, but came up with nothing. Tom's face remained set in a stern expression. He seemed like a stranger. Gone were the twinkle in his dark eyes and the warm smile.

She dreaded the moment when he would drop her off. What if he continued his silence and said nothing more to her? What if he made no further plans to see her?

She felt sick at the thought.

What had she done wrong, she wondered?

She shook her head slightly as she looked out the window of the jeep and watched the landscape fly by in the fading light.

She'd lied. She'd lied to both George and Tom...in the same day. She couldn't remember if she'd actually said she didn't know anyone in Alaska to the other, but the point was the same. She had intended to deceive both of them...especially Tom. She'd never planned to tell him her real reasons for coming to Alaska because she didn't want him to know how pathetically desperate and foolish she had been. She could argue that it was really none of his business, and that was true.

She sighed as she considered Tom, sitting next to her, quiet and withdrawn. She suspected he wasn't forgiving of deceit and lies. She'd made a mistake and she didn't know how to fix it.

They pulled up to the entrance of her hotel. Abbie stalled as she got out of the jeep, hoping Tom would say something.

"Goodnight, Tom," she said quietly, unable to meet his cool eyes.

"Goodnight, Abbie. Take care," he said as he put the jeep in gear.

Abbie stepped away from the vehicle, and Tom pulled out of the parking lot without another word.

****

Tom drove away with resolve. He'd seen the hurt look in Abbie's eyes when he'd dropped her off, but he wasn't going to let himself be swayed by the sadness clouding her beautiful face.

She'd deceived him. He didn't know why she was lying, but it seemed clear that she was hiding something, and it had to do with George. The intimate way the man had grabbed her suggested some sort of relationship.

Tom reminded himself of his promise that morning. He didn't want to go through this sort of thing again. He'd had enough lies with Debbie. He had no intention of falling for a woman who couldn't tell the truth.

Abbie would be hard to forget. She'd been a bit mysterious about her reasons for coming to Alaska, but he'd been so attracted to her that he'd taken what she said at face value.

Tom argued with himself. What if she had just met the guy? What if she didn't know him? He should give her the benefit of the doubt.

The way they'd been talking at breakfast and the proprietary air with which the stranger had grabbed her arm gave Tom the impression that they knew each other well.

He felt he'd given Abbie plenty of opportunity to be open with him, but apparently she decided he didn't need to know, so...he guessed he didn't need to pursue her anymore either.

And what the heck was he doing pursuing her anyway? She was just here for a few days. What was he thinking?

He wasn't thinking...that was the entire problem. He was just reacting. Every time she came near, he couldn't focus on anything else but the way she looked and the way she smelled. He loved to hear her laugh, and he loved the way her eyes sparkled like gold when she was happy.

Tom clenched his jaw. He wanted her with a ferocity that shocked him. It was all he could do today at the concert to stop himself from pulling her down onto the grass next to him and burying his face in her sweet neck and silky hair. He had planned to have dinner with her this evening and then let the night take them where it would. He couldn't deny, even to himself, that he had hoped they would come together in a night of passion.

Instead, he'd walked away. A lump formed in his throat and his chest tightened. It was clear she was hiding something, but he didn't own her. He hardly knew her. She didn't have to tell him every intimate detail of her life just because he wanted to know all about her.

He wished he could trust again like he had when he was younger. Debbie ruined that for him, he thought bitterly. Thoughts of his ex-wife reminded him that he was supposed to meet her for dinner tomorrow night. He wondered what she wanted this time. If it was the same thing she wanted last time, she was going to be out of luck...especially now that he'd met Abbie.

****

Abbie went up to her room and lay down on the bed. She had to talk to someone. She actually felt much worse now than when George had told her not to come...if that was possible. If she had stayed at home, her life would still be boring, but she wouldn't be so sad and depressed.

She dialed her cell phone.

"Hello?"

"Cassie? It's me, Abbie."

"Abbie," the sweet voice on the other end of the line exclaimed. "How are you? Are you in Alaska now? Have you met Mr. Right?"

Abbie started to cry. She couldn't help herself. The

sound of Cassie's sweet, nonjudgmental, and hopeful voice released all the pent-up emotions Abbie had held inside since George rejected her. She told Cassie everything that happened from the time she met Tom on the plane up to the present, leaving out no details. Cassie listened sympathetically, cooing occasionally. When Abbie finally stopped rambling and sobbing, Cassie gently spoke her mind.

"I'm sorry everything seems so messed up, sweetie. I wish I could be there for you, but we just flew in from London." She paused. "Listen, honey, you know I believe in love at first sight. I fell in love with Sanjay when I first saw him, and I don't know why you wouldn't have fallen in love with this guy, Tom, right away—especially if he's as wonderful as you say."

Abbie hiccupped and listened.

"I think you might need to come clean with him if you get the chance. Sanjay and I discovered that our refusal to talk to each other when we were confused and in pain was the one thing that kept us from coming together sooner."

"I know. But what if I don't get the chance to tell him? What if he doesn't call me again? When he dropped me off, it didn't look like he wanted anything to do with me ever again." A hiccup and a sniffle followed.

"Then you'll have to call him," Cassie said firmly. "What are you going to do about George?"

"I don't know. I'm so confused. I don't even know why I agreed to meet him for breakfast. I should have just told him to take a hike...like he basically told me."

"I have to say, Abbie, I don't like the sound of him. Suggesting you have sex with him right away? And then grabbing your arm? He sounds kind of aggressive."

"He does, doesn't he?"

"Well, I'm rooting for Tom—not to influence you or anything," Cassie chuckled.

Abbie responded with a watery laugh.

"You're supposed to be rooting for me. I'm the friend, remember?"

"Oh dear," Cassie clucked sympathetically. "I *am* rooting for you. Of course I am. May the best man win, I say."

Abbie couldn't help but chuckle with her optimistic

friend.

"Just remember, Abbie, love at first sight *does* happen. I know it. It can happen to you. Call Tom."

"Okay, Cassie. Thanks for listening. I'll talk to you soon."

"Keep me posted," Cassie said.

Abbie closed her cell phone and stared at it for what seemed like an hour. She steeled up the courage, opened the phone again, and dialed.

Chapter Seven

Abbie rose early and went downstairs for a quick breakfast. She wanted to get on the road as soon as possible because she had a lot of ground to cover in one day.

Her plan was to drive several hours south to Seward, a small town at the edge of the Kenai Fjords. She hoped to stop along the way and take photographs of some of her favorite sights. The Seward Highway followed the waters of Turnagain Arm southeast before the arm dwindled away to a small river. The highway then led south to the town of Seward on Resurrection Bay. She and the kids often stayed at several streamside campgrounds along the highway as well as in Seward. Abbie had many fond memories of camping with the kids, and she looked forward to taking as many pictures as possible to share with them upon her return.

She packed up maps and extra clothing in the car, though the weather was warm, and set out to cross Anchorage and head south.

Abbie would be on her own today as had been her plan when she first realized she'd be she was going to be alone in Alaska. She stiffened her spine and vowed to get the most out of the day.

Abbie lifted her chin and asserted she wasn't some downtrodden, sad woman who didn't know how to enjoy her own company. In fact, she looked forward to the challenge of touring by herself. Many women did it. She could too!

The trees in the city had turned a bright red-gold, and Abbie admired them, something she was unable to do the day before due to the distraction of Tom's presence. She had a momentary longing to share her joy in the fall colors with him, but quickly suppressed the thoughts. She threw her shoulders back, gave herself a good shake, and gripped the steering wheel with confidence.

She passed Potter Marsh, a wetland of bright red-tipped gold and green grasses and cool waters where geese and ducks paddled lazily. On her right lay Turnagain Arm, the wide body of water which reached inland from Cook Inlet. The tide ran high, and white caps dotted the river, giving it the appearance of a small sea. Snow-capped mountains guarded each side of the inlet as far as the eye could see. Abbie kept her eyes open for whales, either the white bubble heads of the beluga or the jutting black fins of the orca. She had seen both here in the past.

Her first stop was McHugh Creek, fifteen miles outside of Anchorage. Abbie remembered the site with fondness. She'd spent many an hour here trying to capture the gurgling stream and cascading waterfall on camera. In addition, there was a parking lot up above the waterfall where she had once photographed the sweeping views of Turnagain Arm.

She parked the car and followed a paved path to the top where a lone evergreen, bent by the wind, continued to stand after all these years. Happily, her old friend still stood. She had many photos of the sturdy soul. Some things never changed, she sighed contentedly. She left the path and came to stand by the base of the tree to gaze down the length of the wide river as it wove a channel through the mountains in the distant south. The wind on top of the hill blew fiercely and her hair slapped her face, but it was a warm Chinook wind which cleansed and calmed as it buffeted her.

"Well, if you aren't a sight for sore eyes."

Abbie turned quickly to see Tom approaching on the path. His own hair, tied back at the neck, blew in the wind as wildly as hers. Her knees weakened at the sight of the man whose face filled her thoughts, and she reached out to clutch a branch of the tree to steady herself.

"Tom!"

"I'm glad you called. I'm sorry I wasn't home. I tried to call you back this morning, but you had already left."

Abbie fought to keep her hair out of her eyes as she searched his gorgeous face. At the sight of him, she forgot everything she'd told herself about enjoying her solitude.

"I'm glad you told me where you were going. I took a chance that I might catch you here. Everyone stops at McHugh Creek. It's so beautiful," he smiled widely with an expansive gesture of his arms. "And even if you hadn't stopped, I would have seen your car go by on the highway below, and I would have hightailed it out of here to catch up with you."

Abbie's lips quivered into a semblance of a smile. "I'm so glad to see you."

"I'm glad to see you, too. I've been waiting for you down below, hoping I wouldn't miss you." He hesitated as he looked at the mountains across the water. He ran a slow hand through his hair in a futile attempt to smooth it back. "I'm sorry about yesterday. I acted badly. We were supposed to have dinner—you and I," he smiled apologetically at her.

"Oh, that's okay," Abbie placated. "I...I wanted to explain something to you—"

"You don't need to," Tom interrupted. "I shouldn't have behaved the way I did. You have the right to your privacy. I have to admit I got jealous, and I don't have the right to do that. I don't own you," he ended on a firm note.

Abbie's heart flopped in her chest as she listened to his words.

I wish I did belong to you...

"I really think I need to explain myself, Tom," she pressed anxiously.

"Okay, how about later? I'm..." He paused, shoved his hands in his pockets and looked down at the ground for a moment. "I'm afraid you'll say something I don't want to hear. Let's enjoy the day together since I ruined last night. Then, if you still need to explain something to me, you can. Okay?" His worried smile melted her heart.

Abbie didn't want to ruin the day any more than he did, and she suspected he would turn from her if she told him the truth of her trip to Alaska. She couldn't explain about George without revealing the foolish loneliness and desperation that led to her arrival. Tom would think she was ready to latch onto any man who would have her.

Well, aren't you? It sure looks that way.

"Okay, it'll wait," Abbie reassured them both.

Tom smiled gratefully and took Abbie's hand as they

made their way down to the parking lot. They agreed to travel in his jeep and pick up her car on the way back.

Abbie tingled with anticipation at sharing the day with Tom. She had never seen Alaska with an adult companion. Her husband had been out of town too often to camp or fish with the kids and her.

They drove along the highway commenting on the scenery. Abbie admired the improvements made to the road since she'd left. Roadside rest stops had been expanded to include shelters and displays providing information on the surrounding mountains and the local flora and fauna.

At Abbie's direction, Tom pulled into a campground that Abbie adored. It perched on the edge of a glacial creek surrounded by lush green mountains. They wandered down to the edge of the creek, and Abbie rested on a log and took some pictures.

"This place hasn't changed in ten years. I can't believe it," she sighed peacefully. "I loved this campground. There were never very many people here, and we always had the river to ourselves. I used to sit here for what seemed like hours with my binoculars scanning the mountains for Dall sheep or bears, but I never saw any. Still, it's always fun looking, isn't it?"

"Yes, it is," Tom agreed. He stood beside her, hands casually resting in his denim pockets. "You said it was just you and the kids. Did you tent camp?" he asked curiously.

"Well, we tried the first summer we were here, but the kids and I froze at night—even at the height of summer—so I talked my ex-husband into letting me buy a little recreational vehicle. It was a tiny thing, just perfect for the kids and me. We had a great time—cooking, eating, playing games, sleeping. We did a *lot* of sleeping when it rained." Abbie looked up at him and laughed. She had the most embarrassing urge to grab his leg, and rest her face against it, but she restrained herself.

"Didn't your husband ever go camping with you guys?"

"Yes, once, but he was away most of the time, and as you know, there's only a limited amount of time for camping here in Alaska. So, we went by ourselves. There were times, though, I wished I could have had another adult around." Abbie studied the spectacular waterfall streaming down the mountain on the other side of the creek.

Tom laid a gentle hand on the top of her head. Did she dare grab it and cover it with kisses? She managed to control herself and avoid rubbing against his hand like a kitten, although she was sure she heard herself purr.

"Do you enjoy camping, Tom?"

"We camped with our parents when we were kids, although we tended to head north towards my mother's village. And I camped, if that's what one could call it, quite a few times over the years on archaeological digs. Those little trips would last up to six weeks, and I couldn't wait to get home. But, yes, I would say I enjoy camping. I like being outdoors."

"Me too. I love it here." She hugged herself with unrestrained joy.

Tom kneeled down on one knee in front of her in a quick movement and brought her face to his. She welcomed his kiss and put her arms around his neck. As she did so, she lost her balance on the log, and they fell over onto the rounded river pebbles in a tumble of laughter and embarrassment.

"Well, that worked out nicely," Tom laughed as he raised himself to a sitting position. He leaned over to help her up, and they stood together.

Abbie's face burned bright red with embarrassment.

If only I hadn't been so grabby. I'm such a klutz.

Tom leaned in to kiss her lips again, but this time, Abbie kept her arms to herself. He straightened up with a smile and looked at her clasped hands knowingly.

"You can grab me any time, Abbie," he said in sensual husky voice. He reached for her hand and gave it a gentle kiss before he led her back to the car.

****

Tom and Abbie arrived in Seward much later in the day than they expected. End of summer traffic slowed their progress on the two-lane highway, along with frequent stops so Abbie could take pictures. It was almost 4 p.m. when they pulled into the quaint tourist town at the end of the highway.

Tom parked the car, and Abbie made her way to a restroom along the pier. She noted with pleasure that Seward hadn't changed much in the intervening years. Fishermen still cut up their catch of the day, mostly halibut. Seagulls squawked and fought each other for the cast off pieces thrown into the water.

She came out of the restroom and returned to the jeep, but Tom was gone. Assuming he had gone to the restroom as well, she nonchalantly strolled across the tiny main street to browse the window of one of the gift shops. As she admired items in the display window with one eye and kept the other eye on the jeep, she heard Tom's voice nearby. She moved in the direction of his voice, but stopped when she saw him pace back and forth on the side of the building with a cell phone in his hand. Something told her to pull back out of sight.

"No, Debbie, I can't make it for dinner tonight. I'm down in Seward, and I'm not going to make it back in time."

Abbie knew she should give him his privacy and move away. She bit her lip. If she did make a move to leave, he might see her and think she had been deliberately eavesdropping.

"Well, I'm sorry. Maybe we can get together tomorrow night." Another pause and a sigh. "Debbie, we've tried this before. What makes you think it would be any different this time? I haven't changed." He paused again. "Debbie, please don't cry." Another pause. "All right, I'll talk to you tomorrow. It's going to be okay."

Abbie ducked into the store as fast as she could. This must be the ex-wife he was supposed to meet for dinner two nights ago. She couldn't help but be glad she was responsible for their failure to meet tonight. But she felt more than a twinge of guilt that Tom had to cancel his plans. He hadn't said anything about needing to be back in Anchorage early, and she wondered why he'd failed to mention it. Was it possible that he was hiding something from her? According to the phone call, he and his ex-wife were meeting tomorrow. Were they reconciling? If so, why had he kissed her? She wished she knew more about the woman. Tom seemed unhappy to hear from her the other day, yet anxious to meet with her. Was he still in love with his ex-wife?

She watched Tom head back over to the jeep, and she came out of the store and crossed the street to meet him.

"There you are," he smiled.

Abbie returned the smile, but it felt more like a grimace. He confused her, and she didn't understand his motives. The more she thought about it, the more worried she grew that he still loved his ex-wife. And if that were the case, then he shouldn't be making passes at her.

"Let's go get something to eat," he said with a curious look in her direction. They walked back across the street and entered a café next to the gift shop.

Distracted by her thoughts, Abbie barely noticed the quaint small restaurant whose interior décor boasted nautical and fishing themes. The smell of food made her slightly ill, although the restaurant was filled with happy customers.

Silently, she studied the menu without raising her eyes. She knew Tom watched her, but she couldn't think of anything civil to say. She wanted to ask him about his relationship with his ex-wife, but how did one tackle a question like that with any grace?

"Is everything okay?" he asked, cocking his head to one side to see her down turned face.

"Sure." She bared her teeth again in a facsimile of a grin and returned her attention to a menu that appeared to be a blur of writing.

"You seem quiet," he pressed.

"Just tired, I guess," she lied.

"Oh," confusion creased his brow.

Abbie wished he would tell her that he'd had dinner plans or that he'd rescheduled them. She wanted him to be upfront with her. The fact she had not yet been completely honest with him flitted through her mind, and she frowned. She *had* tried to tell him this morning. Maybe she would tell him now.

Why not?

The waitress came to take their order, and when she left, Abbie plunged in.

"Remember, I told you this morning that there was something I wanted to explain?"

"Now?" he asked with a small set smile. "I thought

we were going to wait."

"Now is a good time," she said firmly. "I came up here to Alaska to meet a man."

She paused, building up steam, but she froze when he threw back his head and laughed.

"I have to admit I've heard that before. Lots of women come up here hoping to meet a man because they think there are so many single men up here just pining away for females."

Abbie fumed. He had completely misunderstood what she meant and taken the wind out of her self-righteous sails.

"That's not what I meant," she sputtered.

"Well, you did meet a man, as it happens," Tom said with a sparkle in his eyes as he continued to chuckle. "Me," he tapped his chest. His face darkened a bit as he added, "And the other guy, I guess."

That's the expression she wanted! That furrowed brow, the frown which replaced his irritating grin. She pressed her advantage.

"Yes, the other guy. His name is George. He's the man I came up here to meet," she announced with relish. Not so deep down, Abbie knew she was making a terrible mistake, but she couldn't help herself.

Tom didn't say anything, but his knuckles whitened on his coffee mug. His face smoothed out into a blank expression, but Abbie could see his jaw working.

"I tried to tell you this morning, but you wanted to wait," she said digging deeper.

Tom still didn't respond, and Abbie's well-developed sense of shame threatened to overwhelm her. Her chest tightened and her throat ached, but she refused to give in to tears. He wasn't giving her any satisfaction. She wanted to stay angry at him.

"Well?" she asked, leaning back and crossing her arms.

The waitress brought their food. Tom looked down at his heaping plate and began to eat. Abbie couldn't stomach the sight of hers and left it untouched.

"Well what?" Tom asked between bites. He glanced at her with cool eyes.

"Isn't there anything you want to say...or ask?"

Please tell me about your ex-wife. Say something! Reassure me.

"Not really," he said with a nonchalance that made Abbie cringe.

*He wasn't serious about me at all, was he? Probably can't wait to get back to town and get rid of me.*He continued. "As I said this morning, you're entitled to your own life. I don't own you."

Abbie stared at him with daggers in her eyes.

Tom smiled slightly as he added, "I'm surprised though that you've found so much time to spend with me. I suppose I should be grateful."

"Well—"

"Don't bother to explain anything to me. It's none of my business."

"I...I," Abbie fumed impotently.

"I'm finished here. Do you want to take your food to go?" he asked courteously as he rose to pay the check.

Abbie shook her head mutely. She stood up and marched out the door. A heavy rain had begun to fall. She stalked across the street to the jeep, hoping she could cling to her anger and not give way to the tears which threatened to choke her. She wouldn't give him the satisfaction.

Tom followed, started the car, and pulled onto the road. As they drove out of town, neither one spoke. Abbie kept her eyes fixed on the rain-drenched road. She dared not look at him or she would burst into tears. The steady rhythm of the windshield wipers helped calm her. She tried to think of anything else besides Tom. She thought about Kate and Tim and Cassie. She even thought about her ex-husband, though that did nothing to help dispel her grief.

What had she done? She could have explained better. In fact, she hadn't explained at all. She wondered if she would ever get the chance to tell him why she came to Alaska. Would he even listen to her at this point? Would he care? Probably not, she told herself firmly.

There seemed to be no doubt that he still loved his ex-wife. The man hadn't remarried in twelve years. That had to be unresolved grief...unrequited love. She was sure of it.

Jarred out of her thoughts when Tom's arm suddenly slammed against her chest, she gasped as the jeep slid sideways. Tom managed to straighten the jeep and brought it to a halt. He stared straight ahead. Abbie followed his widened eyes and, through the rain-spattered windshield, made out a slow-moving massive wall of mud and boulders pouring down from the hillside onto the road in front of them. The vehicle had come to a stop about twenty feet behind the debris which spread its thick mass across the road, over the embankment and into the river on Abbie's right.

"Are you all right?" He lowered his arm.

"Yes, I'm fine," Abbie said her anger replaced by a surge of anxiety. "What happened?"

"Mudslide."

Tom jumped out of the jeep to survey the immense mound of mud and debris. Abbie climbed out as well and stared at the damage. A huge section of the hillside had given way, and the mudslide piled over six feet high across the road in places. There was no way through. The road was blocked.

Tom reached for his cell phone. His eyes narrowed.

"No service," he said with a frown and put it away. He turned to study the road to the south.

"Come on, let's head back. They're not going to be able to clear this before morning. We may have to spend the night in Seward," he said grimly.

Abbie dragged herself back into the jeep and watched Tom turn the vehicle around. She was surprised to see no other cars on the road.

Spend the night in Seward? Not with him so unfriendly.

"I can't believe this." Tom brought the car to a halt only a few hundred yards down the road in front of yet another mudslide from the same disintegrating hillside. This one was much smaller than the first, but still impossible for the jeep to traverse.

"Are we stuck?" Abbie asked incredulously.

"It looks that way," Tom muttered. He looked at his watch. "It's getting late. They're not going to bring bulldozers out until morning."

"Even if they know someone's trapped on the road?"

"No, it's too dangerous to try to dig out in the dark. They won't know there's a mudslide on the highway until someone who can't get through reports it. I imagine they'll send a helicopter out to see if anyone was on the road and got trapped under the mud, but there's no room to land here. We're probably not getting out of here until morning."

Tom descended from the vehicle and surveyed the southern mudslide with his hands on his hips. Abbie joined him. She couldn't believe she had bucked at spending the night in Seward.

At least I would have had a warm, dry bed.

She wondered how low the temperature would drop as darkness fell. The rain had lightened to a drizzle, but not before it had done its damage to the hillside.

Tom studied the area, apparently assessing their situation. She could still see the mudslide to the north.

"What if the hillside above us gives way?" Abbie asked with some legitimate concern.

"I hope it doesn't," Tom said grimly as he searched the hillside above the car. "It's mostly rock. I think it's going to be okay. We're going to have to leave the jeep here. I don't really see any place to pull it off the road. There's not much of a shoulder. Besides, it's like our own parking lot, don't you think?" he turned to her with the first smile she'd seen on his face in hours.

"I'd better go see what I've got in the jeep to make us comfortable," he said, walking around to the back and lifting the tailgate. Abbie curiously peered over his shoulder while maintaining her distance. She watched as he sorted through sleeping bags, bottled water, nutrition bars, a cord of wood, cans of soup, matches, and a flashlight. She wasn't surprised to find Tom prepared with the necessities for travel on Alaskan roads.

He seems so...capable.

While Abbie admired him from afar, Tom climbed into the back of the jeep and pushed the rear seat down. He spread the sleeping bags out.

"Well, that looks like where we're going to sleep tonight, I guess," he said, thoughtfully studying his interior design.

Abbie didn't know what to think. She didn't even

know what she felt. Relief? Anxiety? Fear? Anger? Grief? All of them? She was grateful Tom was here. She could just as easily have been trapped here alone if he hadn't shown up, and she didn't have any cold weather gear in her rental car.

She had to admit a certain anxiety at being alone with him all night. She'd done her best to upset him, and he seemed very distant and withdrawn. Quite possibly, he didn't even like her anymore and couldn't wait to see the last of her. Maybe he would have preferred to be stranded with his ex-wife?

Abbie wished she'd never come to Alaska. At that moment, she would be have been tucked in her warm bed and reading some romance novel with a happy ending.

In a huff of her own making, Abbie slipped back into the passenger's seat for shelter from the light drizzle. She watched Tom stroll up and down the road on the side of the river. He seemed to be searching for something. He began collecting rocks and piling them up on the side of the road in a circle. To Abbie, he looked suspiciously like a wilderness scout on a campout.

Unable to contain her curiosity, she stepped out of the jeep to investigate. The rain had stopped, and birds sang in the evergreens by the side of the road. Birds singing? Didn't they know there'd been a mudslide? The serene sound seemed out of place with the destruction of the hillside and blockage of the road both in front and behind the jeep.

Tom worked on building a fire pit, and Abbie heard him humming to himself. He seemed content...as if he were on a family camping trip.

He looked up as she approached.

"I've got some dry wood in the jeep, but I think we'd better see if we can collect more. I don't know how much will be dry after the rain. There might be some under those trees over there," he said and pointed to some evergreens and birches along the road. "Do you want to help me look for some?"

Abbie nodded and headed off to find kindling and dry wood for the fire. She wondered again how cold it would get when the sun went down, and wished she had a dry change of clothes. She also wondered how she would be able to sleep next to Tom in the small vehicle. Maybe she could just sit up in the front seat and doze. She didn't think she could bear the nearness of him. Not if she couldn't have him.

She brought her booty back to the campsite and dropped the wood when she heard the sound of an approaching helicopter. It popped into view above the tree line and hovered. Though the sun was low in the sky and close to setting, she suspected she and Tom were clearly visible to the helicopter crew. Abbie waved her arms overhead, hoping they would land. She saw Tom wave at the helicopter as well, but his gesture seemed to be more of a greeting than a desperate plea for help. The helicopter moved away. Abbie watched it go, knowing Tom's earlier prediction was correct. They would not be dug out until morning. There would be no desperate rescue since they didn't appear to be in danger and the temperature was not expected to reach freezing tonight.

She gathered up the kindling and wood she'd dropped and dropped them by the fire pit. Tom expertly lit the fire and pulled up a large round rock, gesturing for Abbie to sit. She lowered herself onto the impromptu chair and warmed herself by the newborn fire.

Tom sat down across from her and stoked the growing fire.

"I'll bet you wish you'd eaten your food at the restaurant, don't you?" he said with something closely resembling a smirk on his face.

Abbie's spine stiffened.

How dare he?

She armed herself for battle once again.

"Not really," she said with forced nonchalance. "I'm still not hungry," she lied.

"Oh," he grinned at her without the charm of his earlier smiles. "I guess I'll be eating alone tonight, then."

"Maybe so," she retorted.

He poked the now crackling fire with a slight smile on his face. Who knew this sweet man could be so...so...smug?

"I heard you on the phone earlier," Abbie said determined to draw him into a confrontation. Her anxiety compelled her to get his attention, good or bad.

"Oh, really? Were you eavesdropping?" He raised his eyebrows.

"No," she fumed. "I just happened to be standing there. So...you were supposed to meet your ex-wife tonight for dinner. Why didn't you say so earlier? You didn't have to come with me today."

Say something, Tom! Tell me I'm wrong, that you wanted to be with me

"No, I didn't have to come with you today, did I?" he answered shortly. "Maybe your *friend* should have come with you."

His biting sarcasm took Abbie by surprise. The unnatural tone challenged her to aggravate him even further.

"Yes, maybe he should have," she lied. "Or better yet, I should have come on my own. I don't need a man to help me get around. I'm perfectly capable of traveling on my own without any help from anyone," she said defiantly, her eyes flashing.

"You're confusing me, Abbie. I thought you said you came up here to *meet a man*. Now you have two men, and you say you don't need anyone at all. So, why did you come to Alaska?" he asked her pointedly.

Abbie blushed or maybe it was the heat from the fire on her cheeks. She took a stick and poked at the fire.

"Very funny," she fumed. "You don't know anything about me. I don't have to explain why I came up here. That's my business."

"You're right. It *is* your business, just like my phone calls are *my* business."

"Good," she said firmly. "You have your business and I have my business and that's the way it will stay." Abbie stood up and stalked off with a straight back and her head held high. No sooner had she moved away than she wished she had stayed beside the fire. The air grew chillier as the sun set.

She walked up and down the side of the road pretending to search for something. She glanced back occasionally to see Tom getting things out of the jeep. It appeared as though he planned to make supper. Even in her anger, she found him an impressive sight as he opened cans of soup and brought out packages of crackers.

Immensely handsome, yet intelligent and capable. She sighed. He just couldn't be hers, she thought. His cold eyes stared at her flatly, and she knew that meant their short and brief flirtation, if that's what one might call it, had ended

Abbie dashed away a useless tear with the back of her hand. There was nothing she could do about the aching in her throat until it eased.

Tired of her pretense and cold from damp clothes, Abbie swallowed her pride and returned to the fire.

"Cold, huh?" Tom grinned.

Although certain his smile resembled a smirk, Abbie refused to be baited. Defeated, she remained quiet while Tom heated the soup. It smelled delicious. Given her depression, the pangs of hunger surprised her. Tom handed her a can, a spoon, and a package of crackers. Abbie sipped her soup gratefully and ate half the package of crackers. Her body began to thaw as the heat of the soup made its way to her stomach.

The dark night sky made it difficult to see anything outside of the circle of fire. Abbie felt safe though. Predators did not unduly concern her. The fire would keep any curious bears or wolves at a distance, although she suspected most animals had been cut off from this stretch of road by the mudslide as well.

She wasn't alone to face the unknown. Tom sat nearby, reassuring with his calm presence.

She surreptitiously studied his face across the flickering firelight. For what seemed like the hundredth time that day, she speculated on why he had never remarried. Women must fawn over him. She wondered how his female students managed to get through his classes. If she were his student, she would daydream through an entire hour of his lectures listening to his deep voice and wishing his mouth were pressed up against her ear whispering tender words of love.

He finished his soup and put the can down. Abbie watched from under veiled lashes as he took the rubber band out of his pony tail and shook out his wet hair. It fell around his face, giving him a romantic, exotic appearance, enhanced by the flickering light of the fire. She peeked over her can of soup noting that he looked nothing like the staid professors she had studied under.

He caught her looking at him and smiled as color crept up into his cheeks.

"It's wet. I'm trying to get it to dry out."

Abbie nodded, but did not reply. Feeling strangely mute, she struggled against an almost overwhelming compulsion to run her hands through his jet black hair. She wondered if it would feel as silky as it looked.

Was it only a few hours before when he had touched her hair at the river? When he had kissed her? It seemed ages ago—last week, last month, last year. Abbie felt the familiar tightness in her chest as she wondered once again why she had told him about George in such a vicious manner. She hadn't even told him the truth, but had let him believe she had planned on meeting George all along.

George!

He was the furthest thing from her mind as she looked at the face of the man she wanted more than anything in the world. Sighing once again, she stared back down into the fire. She wished the feeling were mutual.

She finished her soup, and Tom picked up the cans and put them into a plastic bag. He took the bag over to the jeep. She knew he was locking up the garbage to avoid attracting wild animals.

He returned to the campsite and sat down again. They passed the time in silence while they relished the remains of the dying fire. All the dry wood had been burnt, or Abbie would have gladly stayed by the fire throughout the night if she could. Anything to avoid getting into the jeep with Tom.

The last embers finally died away, and Tom rose slowly to head back to the jeep. Abbie followed reluctantly.

He opened up the back of the jeep and turned to her. "Abbie, I hate to say this, but I think you should get out of those wet clothes and into the sleeping bag. I'm going to take mine off, so I hope you're not too offended. We can't sleep in these damp clothes. Hopefully, they'll dry out by morning."

Chapter Eight

Abbie stared at Tom, her eyes wide. Take her clothes off? This morning, that might have sounded like the greatest idea in the world, but tonight...? How was she going to sleep next to him naked?

Abbie saw a long sleepless night ahead of her as she struggled to keep from touching him and longing for him to touch her.

He was right though, they couldn't sleep in wet clothes.

"Turn around," she gave in.

While Tom turned around, she quickly slipped out of her jacket, jeans, shirt, shoes, and damp socks and then climbed inside the back of the jeep wearing only her bra and panties. She leaned forward to drape her clothes over the steering wheel and slid down hastily into one of the sleeping bags.

"Okay," she called.

"Turn around," Tom repeated, chuckling as he took off his coat.

Abbie closed her eyes and fervently wished she could watch him shed his clothes. She imagined his brown muscular chest partially covered by the long hair which lay over his shoulders. After he removed his hiking boots, he would unbutton his jeans and let them fall. A small sigh escaped her lips.

She heard the back of the jeep close and felt his warm body as he climbed in next to her. She opened her eyes in the dark and studied him as he laid his clothes out on the dashboard. The clouds had given way to moonlight, and Abbie could see the strong jut of his chin, the way his hair fell over his face, and the narrowness of his waist below his broad shoulders.

When he lay next to her, she turned on her side and inched as far as possible to her side of the jeep. In the confined space of the small area, her nose was deliciously tickled by the fresh scent of shampoo in his still damp hair. She breathed in deeply, savoring Tom's essence

He adjusted himself several times trying to get comfortable.

"Abbie, I don't know what's been going on with us today, but I'm too tall to lie on my back in this small space. I'm going to have to lie on my side with my legs bent. That means I'll be spooning with you. I hope you don't mind," he whispered as he found a more comfortable position.

Abbie refused to respond. She felt the warmth of his chest on her back. She held herself rigid and taut as her imagination flooded her mind with images of their bodies intertwined in a passionate embrace. Her body betrayed her, and it took all her willpower to stop herself from turning around and joining with him—whether he desired her or not. She wanted him more than anything in the world, and every part of her body screamed for mercy.

She smothered her face in the sleeping bag.

"Abbie?" he whispered softly as he moved her hair away from his face. "Are you comfortable?"

Abbie nodded her head in the most foolish lie of her life. Yes, she was comfortable. So comfortable she thought her heart might give out. Why couldn't she just turn to him and make him love her? Couldn't he feel how right their bodies fit together? His body molded to hers like a glove.

Abbie started counting sheep. By the time, she reached 400, she felt her body begin to relax. At 750, she let the sheep stop jumping and simply let them wander away into a green field of grass...where she and Tom slept in each other's arms.

****

Tom gritted his teeth. The warmth of Abbie's body was agonizing. It was all he could do not to flip her over and pull her toward him. He wondered if she could sense his arousal or even returned it. How could she not? Their bodies seemed made for each other. They were a perfect match.

He longed to touch her hair shimmering in the moonlight but dared not. What had gone wrong today? Something had happened, and she had done her best to hurt him. He wasn't certain who this guy, George, was or what was going on between them, but she had this angry gleam in her eyes that made him think she deliberately tried to upset him. Unfortunately, she had succeeded.

The phone call!

Debbie's phone call. Abbie said she'd heard him on the phone. What could she have heard that would have made her mood change like that?

He tried to remember what he'd said on the phone. Debbie wanted to come back...again. They'd tried to reconcile about a year after she left the first time, but she'd taken off again a few months later. This was the fourth or fifth time she'd asked him to take her back. Even though he had refused her every time, he needed to bring out the big guns and firmly tell her no—convince her that he was never going to reconcile with her...never.

Tom knew he'd been too passive with her in an effort to avoid hurting her feelings. He'd known the woman for years. She manipulated people, had always manipulated him. He needed to firmly convince her that he was never going to reconcile.

Tom knew he didn't love his ex-wife anymore, and he hadn't for years. He hoped he'd never had to actually say those words to her. He didn't want to hurt her further, because he believed Debbie loved him in her own way. She just wasn't capable of being faithful to one man. She grew bored easily. He knew she'd had a number of love affairs over the last twelve years. Hadn't she called him in tears over several of them, asking for his advice and sympathy?

Tomorrow night, when he met her for dinner, he would tell her firmly he would never reconcile with her, and he would make sure she believed him.

He stared at the outline of Abbie's body. He could feel her body relax and hoped she had fallen asleep. He suspected he would be awake all night. There was no way he'd be able to sleep with the feel of her sweet skin next to his. He wanted her so badly. He wanted to bury his face in her clean hair and nuzzle the soft skin at the nape of her neck. He wanted to run his hands over her body and imprint himself on her. He wanted to feel her body under his as he made sweet tender love to her.

Tom gritted his teeth and forced his thoughts away from his vision of Paradise. He had to calm down. He pulled away from Abbie's warmth as much as possible in the small vehicle and searched his mind for distractions.

Who was this guy she said she had come to meet? Why had she lied about it? Something was going on, and it wasn't as straightforward as Abbie had made it sound. She'd looked displeased when the fellow had grabbed her arm at the fair. If she came to Alaska to meet the guy, why wasn't she with him? *How do I fit into all of this?*

Tom clenched his jaw at the thought of the two of them together. Whatever the story, he was glad Abbie was here with him—where she belonged. If only she wanted to be here with him.

****

When Abbie opened her eyes in the morning, she found Tom's arms wrapped snugly around her with her hands clasped over his. She didn't move for a long while as she breathed in his scent. His dark hair intertwined with her gold hair, and the mass must have kept both of their faces warm in the night.

She heard Tom's breathing change, and she held her breath, hoping he wouldn't wake up just yet. Reality could stay gone for a while. His face nestled against her back, and his breath warmed the nape of her neck. She longed to back up into him and bury herself even deeper within his arms.

Abbie looked up at the dawn sky. She was in love. She was absolutely sure of it. If she could lie in his safe arms for the rest of her life, she would be the happiest woman on earth.

But she wasn't going to be the happiest woman on earth, was she? It sounded like he was still in love with his ex-wife, and that woman was here to take him back.

A peaceful resignation washed over Abbie as she realized why she'd been so hateful to Tom yesterday. Jealousy. She feared losing him to his ex-wife. But she'd already lost him, hadn't she? She'd made sure of that.

She lay perfectly still in his arms and watched birds circle overhead in the early morning mist, accepting that she might never again have the chance to feel his skin against hers She was grateful to have these few precious minutes.

She closed her eyes drowsily and fell asleep again.

****

The sound of heavy equipment broke the peaceful silence of the morning and woke both Abbie and Tom with a start.

"Good morning," Tom whispered in her ear.

Abbie kept her back to him, afraid he would see the longing in her eyes.

"Morning," she murmured.

He removed his arms from around her without a word and leaned over to get his clothing. Abbie stayed still, wishing she were still cocooned in his arms. She shivered as she felt suddenly bereft, cold, and alone.

Abbie peeked over the edge of the sleeping bag at Tom as he jumped out of the jeep to throw on his shirt and pull on his jeans. His hair had dried, and she watched tenderly as he impatiently brushed it away from his face. As beautiful as it was, he looked like he wasn't used to wearing it down. She remembered its clean scent and the warmth it had provided in the night.

As he moved away to the tree line, Abbie reached for her own clothing. It was stiff with cold, but dry. She crawled out of the back of the jeep and pulled on her rigid jeans, cold shirt, and jacket. She slipped her feet into her shoes and headed in the opposite direction from Tom. She couldn't see any of bulldozers or workers yet, so she suspected they had time.

When she returned to the jeep, Tom leaned against the rear door with his face raised toward the sun.

Abbie followed his eyes skyward. She had to admit the day promised to be beautiful. The sun had begun to dispel the early morning mist. The glorious fall foliage of the surrounding trees shone brightly against the sedate dark colors of the evergreens.

"It looks like they're plowing through from both sides with bulldozers," Tom said with an unreadable glance in her direction. "Hopefully, we'll get out of here soon."

Abbie couldn't bear to hear him say it in just that way. *Hopefully, we'll get out of here soon.* A normal wish for two people trapped by a small disaster now rang like a death sentence. She yearned only to be with him as long as possible anywhere in the world—even stuck on a road between two mudslides.

She turned away and walked toward the front of the vehicle to watch the bulldozers working their magic on the debris up ahead.

"Look, they're breaking through," Abbie called out and pointed to the mudslide to the north. The shovel of the heavy equipment had made an opening large enough for the car to pass through. A highway crew member signaled them forward, and Tom and Abbie jumped into the jeep and made their way through the hole dug out by the bulldozer.

"I thought that would take longer," Tom said as he looked in his rearview mirror. "I'd just been thinking about putting on a pot of coffee to warm up. Good thing I didn't," he said with a brief polite smile.

She returned the smile and looked quickly away at the road ahead. She didn't trust herself not to beg him to love her as she had fallen in love with him. A mantra kept running through her head.

Please love me, please love me.

It was driving her crazy. She pressed her lips tightly together hoping the plea wouldn't accidentally erupt from her mouth.

She knew Tom glanced at her occasionally, but she refused to meet his gaze. What if he saw the longing in her eyes? What if he saw the love? She couldn't bear to see him turn from her. She shook her head slightly and stared out of the passenger's window. The passing scenery flashed by in a blur.

She felt so foolish. How could she have fallen in love so quickly? Normal people didn't do that...did they?

Abbie remembered Cassie's animated face as she described how she and her husband had fallen in love at first...or was it second sight? Cassie was the exception though. Who wouldn't love her? She was so fiercely loyal to those she loved.

Abbie sighed. No, she wasn't Cassie. She was just a pathetically lonely woman who'd been on her own for a long time and was ready to fall in love with the first man who smiled at her. That knowledge didn't change the fact that she was in love. It just showed how silly she was.

What sensible woman falls in love with a man who is still in love with his ex-wife?

****

Tom and Abbie stopped for breakfast at a small café in a little town some distance north of the mudslide. The intimate diner was cozy and warm, and Abbie ate the hot breakfast with gratitude.

She kept her eyes on her coffee mug and her food and answered only when spoken to. Tom finally gave up trying to talk to her and fell silent himself. The quiet seemed worse for the knowledge that her muteness created it, but she simply had nothing appropriate to say. She kept her lips locked against the pleas and screams and wails possessing her mind.

The drive back to Anchorage continued in silence. Abbie berated herself for the waste of precious time with him. But what could she say?

I love you?

That wasn't going to happen. She wasn't going to put either one of them in a miserable position where she begged for his love and he, kindly but firmly, told her that she had rushed or misunderstood or become too emotional or that he was in love with someone else.

He dropped her off by her car at McHugh Creek. To her surprise, he didn't immediately drive away but waited.

"I'll follow you back to town." He stared at some distant spot over her shoulder.

"No need. I'm fine." She would have given anything for him to look at her face, to meet her eyes and tell her...what? That he was in love with her?

"I'll follow you back to town," he repeated in a monotone.

Abbie acquiesced and climbed into her car. She drove the short distance back to Anchorage, wondering if her last sight of him would be in her rear view mirror. She parked at the hotel, and Tom pulled in behind her and waited.

Abbie climbed out of her car and turned to him.

"Take care." He gave her a brief nod and headed out of the parking lot.

"Tom." Her voice broke when she called after his

retreating car. He didn't stop. She had no way of knowing whether he'd heard her call or not. She had no idea what she would say if he stopped.

Abbie fought the overwhelming urge to run after his jeep, screaming for him to return to her. Her throat ached miserably from the tears she held back. She dragged herself up to her room in a daze and let herself in. Everything looked just the same as when she had left it, but everything felt completely different. She was different. She was in love, and the pain seemed like it would never end.

The message light blinked on her phone, but Abbie ignored it. Tom said he'd called yesterday morning, but she doubted he would have called in the last few minutes. She didn't care about any other messages. She might listen to his message later, just to hear his voice when the longing to see him became too much to bear.

She ran a hot bath and sank into it. Closing her eyes, she wished her plane reservations were in one hour instead of day after tomorrow.

****

Abbie heard the phone ringing. Her heart jumped, and she rolled over on the bed and grabbed for it. Tom, maybe it was Tom, she thought with excitement. She looked at the clock. It was late afternoon. She had slept the entire day away.

"Hello," she said breathlessly. *Please, please, please.*

"Abbie? It's George. Where have you been? I've called and left several messages." His voice was gruff.

"George," she repeated mechanically as she wondered where Tom was and what he was doing. "I'm sorry. I've been busy," she murmured.

"Oh, I see. Too busy to return calls?" His tone bordered on sarcastic, and Abbie supposed she deserved it, though she really didn't care.

"I'm sorry, George. What can I do for you?" she asked, wishing he would leave her alone. Tom hadn't called. What else mattered?

"Well, I thought we were supposed to get together yesterday. How about dinner tonight? We're sort of running out of time," he said with a short laugh.

Time for what? Abbie wondered. *He didn't mean....Oh*

no, that wasn't going to happen...ever.

"Yes, I'm going back home soon." *I can't wait to leave.*

"So? What about dinner? Sara called me to find out how things were going. I'd better tell her something or she'll never forgive me."

Sara. What would she tell Sara when she got back? *I fell in love with someone else while I was there. No, no, I just met him on the plane. Yes, that quick! Sounds silly, doesn't it? Your cousin? Oh, I ignored him and spent all my time chasing after this other guy. Him? Oh, it seems he's still in love with his ex-wife.*

She owed Sara better than that. Maybe not George, but definitely Sara. Besides, it looked like she was going to be alone tonight—with plenty of time to think about Tom and his ex-wife. Would they sleep together? Her knuckles turned white as her grip tightened on the phone.

"Uh...sure, George. What time?"

"I'll pick you up at seven. Okay?"

"Seven. That sounds fine. I'll see you then."

She hung up the phone and stared at it. The message light continued to blink, but she didn't want to listen to any of the messages. Obviously, most of them had been from George. She didn't think she could handle hearing Tom's message from yesterday morning right now. Where was he? What was he doing today? Was he with his ex-wife?

Abbie rose from the bed to dress with little care for what she wore. She found herself with time on her hands and strolled down to the creek while she waited for George to arrive. The tide was just coming in, and the fishermen anxiously lined up along the edge casting their lures into the shallow water. She made her way to the walking bridge and looked down into the water. From this vantage point, she could see the large bright red fish working their way up the creek, but the fishermen at the water's edge did not have the advantage of the overhead view. At any rate, the fish had to take the bait in their mouth. They couldn't be taken if they were snagged. She watched as one lucky...or unlucky fisherman stepped into the water in his waders and removed the hook from the back fin of an immense struggling fish. He released the fish back into the stream.

She checked her watch. A few minutes before seven. Was Tom meeting his ex-wife now? Would they return to his house? She didn't even know where he lived. Abbie's stomach twisted into a knot as she tried to imagine what was happening. Why couldn't she tear her mind away from him? What he did was his business. He wasn't hers, and he never had been. A few kisses did not constitute a grand love affair, she lectured herself. *Let it go.*

George arrived just as she returned to the hotel. When he got out of his truck to open the door for her, she found to her surprise that he cleaned up well when he wore attractive clothing.

His light blue shirt contrasted well with his auburn hair. He wore a dark pair of slacks and black dress shoes. Even his mustache and beard had been trimmed, though she still had difficulty reading his face through the facial hair.

"Well, we finally get together," he said with what she thought was a small smile as he closed the door behind her.

"Yes, Sara will be happy," Abbie responded. What made her say that, she wondered? How rude.

Abbie fought an overwhelming desire to run up to her room and jump into bed to bury her head under the covers. She didn't think it was because of George, necessarily. She just didn't want to see anyone right now—not until this night had passed. Would Tom call her tomorrow? Would she ever hear from him again?

"Yeah, I'm sure she will." George made no comment on Abbie's distant tone. "So, where were you yesterday?" he asked as he drove away from the hotel.

"Uh...Seward. I spent the night down there." It was none of his concern.

"Oh really. That's such a touristy town, isn't it? Full of gift shops and cruise ships. I prefer the woods north of Anchorage myself. Less visitors."

Abbie glanced quickly over at him. His face was unsmiling, serious.

"I love Seward," she said somewhat defiantly. "It's so beautiful, nestled in the mountains at the entrance to the Fjords. I think there's a lot more to Seward than just tourists and cruise ships. I have nothing but good memories of it."

"Well, you *are* a tourist," he pointed out with a brief flash of teeth.

"I see," she said. This was going to be a long night. *Sara, Sara, why aren't you here? Do you even know your cousin?*

"By the way, who was that guy at the fair? I've been meaning to ask you. I thought you said you didn't know anyone up here anymore. You looked pretty chummy with him."

"He's just a friend, that's all." Abbie's jaw tightened as she had no intention of continuing with this line of questioning.

"So, you're not going to tell me." He threw her a frown.

"I just did. He's a friend," she answered shortly.

"Where did you meet?" he persisted.

"On the plane."

"Wow, you work fast!"

Abbie swung her head to glare at him.

"Look, George. I don't need that kind of comment from you. I'm free to see whom I want, when I want."

"Okay, okay," he backed off. "Sorry. I didn't mean anything."

Abbie didn't respond. She knew just what he meant.

"Still—" he began.

"Stop," she said firmly.

They arrived at the restaurant which was a Chinese buffet, sporting typical Asian

decor: softly painted wall murals of Chinese mountains and rivers, hanging paper lanterns with red tassels, accent colors of red and gold. They were seated in a red vinyl booth, and Abbie hated the thought of sitting across from George for the entire meal.

She realized now that meeting him for dinner had been a mistake. He was a different man than she had talked to on the phone. Or maybe he wasn't. Maybe she'd been too desperate to really hear the truth. Since she'd met him face to face, she'd found him to be rude, pushy, arrogant, and uncouth. It seemed hard to believe he was Sara's cousin. How could their parents be related?

Abbie rubbed her forehead, too tired and emotionally

drained to worry about his upbringing. A headache seemed imminent.

As she remembered from their phone conversations, George's fondest subject was himself, and she let him talk on and on about his experiences in Alaska and his love of cars. He didn't seem to notice her silence, and she made a pretense of chewing food as often as possible to avoid responses to his comments. It proved unnecessary since he didn't actually ask her any questions.

The interminable dinner finally ended, and they headed back to George's truck. Dusk settled upon the city, and Abbie couldn't wait to get back to her room so she could wallow in self-pity under the covers of her bed.

"Do you want to get a drink?" George asked as he got in the driver's seat.

"No, thanks, George. I really need to get back."

"Why?"

"Because...well, because I need to, that's all," she replied with no ready excuse.

"Well, how about stopping by my place? I could make some coffee. It's on the way back."

"No, thanks, George, I really can't."

He drove out of the parking lot and turned onto the street.

"So, that's it? That's all?" he asked in a gruff voice.

Abbie turned to him, but he kept his eyes on the road.

"I don't know what you mean."

"So, I drop you off. I don't think I'm going to hear from you again. You've found this other guy, and you're not interested in me anymore. Is that the deal?"

"I...I'm sorry, George. This doesn't have anything to do with anybody else. I'm just tired, that's all."

"I don't believe you."

Abbie realized he wasn't heading back to the hotel, but had turned down some streets she was unfamiliar with.

"Well, you should believe me, George." She peered out the window intently. "George, where are you going?"

"I just thought I'd swing by my house and pick up a jacket. I'm going out after I drop you off. You don't mind, do you?"

"Yes, I do mind, George. I told you I don't want to go to your house, and I want you to take me back to the hotel now."

"No, you don't," he said with a small show of teeth under his mustache. "You came all the way up here to see me, so...let's just go to my place and see what we have in common."

A sense of foreboding gripped Abbie.

"George, I said no. Take me home or stop the car and let me out."

"Come on, Abbie. What am I going to tell Sara?" he wheedled. "That we had dinner once?"

"I don't care what you tell her. She's going to find out what you're like from me. Now, take me back to the hotel or stop the car. Now!" Abbie heard the shrillness in her voice that betrayed her growing fear.

George pulled the car into a small parking lot of what looked like a day park. Abbie's heart raced.

"What are you doing?" she asked with a shaky voice.

"You told me to stop the car, and I did. This is fine," he said as he looked around at the empty park. He reached over and pulled Abbie to him.

Before she realized what he was doing, he kissed her. She couldn't breathe, and she twisted her head away and fought to push him back. His arms held her like a vice. Rising panic threatened to overwhelm her.

"George, let me go! Let me go," she managed to beg as he bent his head to hers once again. She was drowning in a sea of scratchy facial hair and teeth as he ground his mouth into hers. She twisted away once again. Her mouth hurt. Her ribs ached where he crushed her to him. She couldn't breathe.

"George, stop. Please stop," she pleaded. A sob escaped her lips.

Don't lose control, Abbie. You have to stay in control.

She fell back against the passenger's door as he abruptly released her and threw her from him. Her head hit the window.

"Ow," she cried.

"For crying out loud! Get out of the truck then. That's what you want," he said in a disgusted voice. "You're some kind of tease, you know that? I was right about you. You *are* a goody two-shoes, frigid woman. I could tell by the phone calls. No wonder you come all the way to Alaska to get a man. You must think we're desperate up here. Well, let me tell you, lady. I can have plenty of women. I don't need you. Get out."

Abbie needed no further urging. She grabbed her purse and jumped out of the car. She ran toward the darkened park. Behind her, she heard George spin his tires and tear out of the parking lot.

When she could no longer hear his engine, she stopped running and found a nearby bench where she sat down heavily. She threw her arms across her chest and hugged herself tightly to control her shaking. She'd never felt so helpless as when George held her against her will. She never wanted to experience that terror again.

Abbie's eyes searched the park. The evening shadows grew large. She felt exposed and vulnerable in the desolate park. It didn't appear to be a very safe place. She needed to get out of the dark and into a more populated area. Where was she? She got up for a better view of the sign with the name of the park. Greenfield Park. Maybe she could call a taxi to come pick her up.

She dug in her purse for her cell phone. As she pulled it out, she noticed her wallet wasn't in her purse. Had it been stolen? Had George taken it?

Abbie weakly dropped down on the bench. Her shaking knees wouldn't support her. She remembered now that she had left her wallet in Tom's jeep when they stopped for breakfast. How could she be so stupid? All her money and her credit cards were in that wallet. What would she pay a taxi driver with? What was she going to do? Tears of frustration burned in her eyes.

She rose from the bench slowly. She'd better start walking, that was if her knees would hold her up. Things could be worse. Anything was better than another minute with George. She had been so wrong about him. Did Sara know what he was like? Abbie seriously doubted that. Abbie tentatively wandered down the road for 100 yards before realizing she didn't know where to go. None of the street names seemed familiar. She supposed she could knock on someone's door, but the neighborhood seemed rundown and dilapidated. She would still have no money to get home.

The late Alaskan dusk brought more shadows. The isolation of the nearby park grew more frightening. What if there were worse things than George?

Abbie heard steps running up behind her. She turned quickly to ward off the attack.

Chapter Nine

A large, yellow, Labrador retriever ran up to her and barked, his tail wagging excitedly.

Abbie sat down on the ground abruptly. Her legs simply would not hold her any longer. She began to laugh and cry as the friendly dog circled her happily, occasionally stopping to try to lick her face.

She reached out to pet the dog searching for the comfort of a warm being. In the distance, she heard a voice. She couldn't see where it came from, but the dog ran off in the direction of the voice. Then she heard a door slam, and she felt completely and utterly alone as she sat on the edge of the darkened park.

She hugged her knees and rested her aching head on her bent arms for a few minutes while she tried to make a plan. Her brain failed the task. She just couldn't think straight.

She heard a vehicle approach and saw George's truck come to a halt near where she sat. Abbie jumped up, clutching her purse, prepared to run back into the shadows of the park.

"Relax, Abbie. I'm not going to hurt you." George spoke in a mocking voice. Belligerent eyes stared at her.

To Abbie's relief, he remained in the truck. No fool though, she backed up a few steps to put distance between George and herself.

"Come on, Abbie, let me give you a ride back to the hotel," he wheedled. "Sara will kill me if she finds out about this."

Abbie shook her head in an odd combination of disgust and wonder. He was worried about Sara? Didn't he have any conscience?

"No, I'm fine," she said with a firm, loud voice as she crossed her arms defiantly. "I'm going to call a cab."

"Come on, Abbie. This is silly." He tried a grin, but it fell short.

"No. Please leave."

"Well, I'm not gonna beg. I've got better things to do than baby sit you. Are you sure?" he asked coldly as he put the truck in gear.

Abbie gave a vigorous nod, fervently wishing he would drive off and leave her to the desolate park which frightened her less than he did.

He did drive off, and Abbie sank back to the curb, her head resting on her knees once again. What was she going to do? She wished the dog would come back to share its warmth and friendliness. Maybe she could follow it home this time. And do what? Borrow money from his owner for a taxi? Not likely...not in this neighborhood, she thought morosely.

Abbie felt the cell phone in her hand vibrate. What if it was George again? She couldn't bear it. He didn't have her cell phone number, did he? Unless Sara gave it to him?

She answered the phone hesitantly.

"Hello?"

"Abbie?" It was Tom. She didn't know how he he'd gotten her phone number, and she didn't care. She started crying and speaking at the same time.

"Abbie. Slow down. I can't understand what you're saying. Are you all right?" he asked urgently.

"I'm sorry. I can't stop crying. I'm alone out here and it's dark and I'm scared," she sobbed. "I don't have my wallet, and I don't have any money, and I don't even know where I am," she wailed pitifully.

"Abbie. What happened? Where are you?" Tom's voice deepened as he pressed her for answers.

"I don't want to tell you what happened. Can you come get me? My wallet is in your car. I'm sorry to bother you. I'm so glad you called. If I could just get my wallet, I'll call a taxi. I promise."

"Where are you?" he demanded.

"I'm at a park on the corner of Brinkley and Temple roads. Do you know where that is? I don't."

Abbie felt like an orphan as she sat on the ground crying into the telephone. She desperately wished the dog would come back to sit beside her.

"Yes, I can find it. I'm in town, so it won't take me

long. Are you safe? I'm going out to the jeep now."

"I don't know. It's very spooky here. I don't know what kind of area this is."

"Okay, I'll stay on the phone while I drive."

"Okay," she hiccupped.

"What happened? Can you tell me?"

Her defenses down and afraid of the dark unknown, accompanied by the occasional sniffle, Abbie told Tom the entire story of her long distance conversations with George, how he had asked her to come up to Alaska and then rejected her when she told him she was on her way. She told him about the nonrefundable airline tickets and meeting George for breakfast. As if she confided in her best friend, she told Tom about accepting George's dinner invitation and his assault on her and abandonment in the park. She told him sheepishly that she had sent George away when he came back to offer her a ride.

Tom didn't interrupt, although she heard an occasional clearing of his throat and a sharp intake of breath as she described the incident in the truck.

"It really wasn't all that bad, Tom. I'm probably exaggerating because I'm upset."

"Don't downplay it, Abbie. I doubt if you're exaggerating. How are you doing? I'm almost there."

"I'm fine," she said in a small voice as she wondered what he thought of her now, especially after she had told him that her original intent on coming to Alaska was to meet George. She couldn't read his voice.

Where was his ex-wife? Had he left her somewhere so he could come to Abbie's rescue?

"Tom?"

"Yes, dear?"

Abbie was momentarily distracted by the endearment. The darkness around her grew more oppressive.

"Why did you call me anyway?"

"Let's talk about that later. I'm on your street."

Abbie saw his jeep pull near, and she jumped up and waved to him. She felt instantly safe. He was her hero in every way, and she knew no man would ever touch her heart the way he did.

He pulled the jeep to the side of the road, got out, and

walked swiftly up to Abbie. Before she knew it, he enveloped her in a warm embrace as he pressed her head to his chest. She clung to him and begged herself not to start crying again as she listened to the rapid pounding of his heart beneath her ear.

He set her back and looked sternly at her. She dreaded his next words.

"Are you all right?" he said as he checked her over.

No lecture. Relief swept through her as she nodded silently. She was spent from pouring out her heart on the phone. Now that he was here in the flesh, she felt foolish and embarrassed. What did he think of her now?

"Let's go," he said firmly as he led her to the vehicle and carefully put her in the passenger's seat. With a nurturing touch, he reached over and pulled her seatbelt around her.

They drove away, and Abbie closed her eyes to relax, but images of George's face looming over hers and the roughness of his arms flooded her mind. She popped her eyes open in hopes the visions would disappear.

For the second time that night, Abbie realized she was being driven to some place other than her hotel, but this time she knew no fear.

"Where are we going, Tom?"

"I'm taking you home with me. I think you need a cup of hot chocolate, a warm fire, and some security."

"Oh," she said meekly. A cup of hot chocolate sounded wonderful, and any extra time spent in his company would be more than she had hoped for. Would his ex-wife be there?

To Abbie's surprise, they drove out of the city to the north. It had never occurred to her that he lived out of town. After twenty minutes on the highway, he pulled off onto a graded road and drove another ten minutes into some woods. It was too dark to see the surrounding landscape other than the tall pine trees, and she wondered where he lived.

Tom pulled up to the front of a well-lit log cabin with a wraparound front porch. He came around, opened her door, and led her up wide wooden steps to the solidly built pine front door. As he pushed open the door, two black and white huskies with startling ice blue eyes greeted them silently, tongues lolling in joy, tails wagging happily. Tom reached down to pat their heads and shoo them back from the door.

"Get back, guys. Let us in."

So, he has dogs. She wondered why he hadn't mentioned the dogs and who took care of them while he was away. How had the dogs fared last night when Tom couldn't return because he'd been trapped by the mudslides?

He stood back to let Abbie enter. She paused at the entrance, instantly charmed by the inside of his home. The décor resembled his character: handsome, masculine, open, and comfortable. Shelves filled with books lined the walls and flanked a floor to ceiling river rock fireplace that dominated the far wall. Several dark green couches surrounded a well-worn red oriental carpet in the middle of the room. A knotted pine coffee table graced the center of the carpet and a dark brown overstuffed easy chair faced the fireplace. She could see a kitchen off to the right and a hallway leading away from the main room, presumably to the bedrooms and the bathroom.

Tom took her jacket and hung it on a wooden coat tree inside the front door. He indicated she should sit on one of the couches as he walked over to the fireplace and quickly lit a fire. She sat down and watched him with loving eyes. When he turned around, she dropped her revealing gaze.

"I'm going to go make that hot chocolate now," he said with a smile. "The bathroom is just down that hall on the right if you need it." He made his way to the kitchen with the dogs padding silently along behind him.

Abbie went down the hall toward the bathroom. An open door led to a bedroom at the end of the hall diagonal to the bathroom. She paused to study it. The bedroom light was off, but the overhead light from the hallway illuminated much of the room. From what she could see, the room had a masculine flavor with a large bed supported by a rustic hand-hewn wooden headboard. The bedspread was chocolate brown, the pillowcases a neutral beige. Several well-stocked bookshelves lined the walls in the bedroom as well. Tom's bedroom!

Had his ex-wife been here, she wondered? Had she

been in that bed? Had they once shared this home? Abbie gave herself a quick shake. There was no point in torturing herself. It was unkind. She stepped into the bathroom and turned on the lights.

The room was clean, and the porcelain looked fresh, bright and new. As she vigorously scrubbed her hands and face to rid herself of the taste and feel of George, she studied the room. No feminine products rested on the shelves. She smiled. It wasn't much, but for a woman in love and desperate for any scrap of hope, significant. The lack of women's toiletries didn't prove that he wasn't reconciling with his ex-wife or that he returned Abbie's feelings in the least, but she smiled nonetheless.

She returned to the living room and sat down on one of the green couches just as Tom emerged from the kitchen with two mugs of steaming hot cocoa. He set them down on the coffee table in front of the couch and sat down in the oversized easy chair across from Abbie.

The dogs came over to Abbie and pushed cold wet noses against her hands. She rubbed the special spot behind their ears while they gazed at her with wide-eyed trust.

"Boy, they're friendly, aren't they?" she smiled shyly at Tom who watched his pets indulgently. "What happened to them last night when you couldn't get back?" she asked curiously.

He grinned. "Yeah, they love visitors. They don't see too many." He paused. "They have a big dog door they can go in and out of. I always leave plenty of food out, so I knew they'd be okay. It's a good thing we weren't gone another night though. Their food bowls were empty when I got home this morning."

He called the dogs over to sit by him, and Abbie leaned forward to pick up her mug. She wracked her brain for another conversation opener as she sat back on the couch to study the living room. With forced nonchalance, she asked, "So, how long have you lived here?"

He followed her eyes around the room as if seeing it from an outsider's view.

"Oh, about five years. I got a great deal on the land here and had the cabin built. There's a lake in back. You can't see it right now because it's dark, but you'll be able to see it in the morning."

In the morning. Abbie savored the words. *In the morning,* she repeated silently. Then she would be here all night. Her face flushed, and she focused her attention on her mug of cocoa.

"How are you feeling?" he asked in a quiet voice.

"Good. I'm much better. I...I'm really sorry about all the crying and sobbing. It's not really like me. I just fell apart, and I don't know why." Abbie kept her eyes on her mug, embarrassed by the hysterical behavior that brought him out into the night to *rescue* her.

"Abbie. Don't." He leaned forward in his chair, his gaze intent. "Don't say you're sorry. Not to me. You've been through a pretty tough experience, not to mention the rough conditions of the night before."

She glanced at him. He settled back into his chair and stared at the fire with a frown on his face.

"I just wish I could do something about this guy, George. Mauling you and leaving you out in the dark like that! I hope you tell your friend, Sara, about him because she shouldn't send any other women his way. I think he's likely to end up in jail soon if he keeps this sort of thing up. I doubt if this is the first time he's done something like this. You were lucky."

"I know," she said meekly. "I *was* lucky. I shouldn't have made such a big deal about it."

"Abbie!" He stood. "I don't mean you did anything wrong. This wasn't your fault. Remember that. He wasn't some stranger. He was supposed to be the family member of a trusted friend. You didn't do anything wrong. And you *should* have made a big deal about it. And I'm glad I could come to pick you up. If anything, I feel like I'm to blame. I shouldn't have left you alone so that you ended up with this guy."

While he spoke, he'd come over to sit next to her on the couch. He put his arm around her shoulder and drew her head to his chest comfortingly. At his last words, Abbie sat upright and stared at him.

"Tom! It's not your responsibility to take care of me. I hope you don't think that." Abbie looked back down at her hands in embarrassment. "Of course, begging you to come get me out of my predicament wasn't the best way to show that you don't have to baby sit me." She gave him a rueful smile, her cheeks high with color.

Tom pulled her gently back into the crook of his arm. She allowed herself to relax into the comfort of his safe embrace.

"I know you're not my responsibility, Abbie." Tom reached down with a gentle touch to turn her face toward him. "I just wish you were," he sighed as he leaned down and kissed her on the forehead.

Abbie's heart skipped a beat when she saw his mouth near her face. *He's going to kiss me*! Her short-lived elation died when he stopped at her forehead. The sweetness of the featherlike kiss on her brow touched her. Ashamed of herself, she tried to swallow her disappointment. She had expected more...wanted more. She lowered her head once again to hide the longing in her eyes.

"Abbie?" His husky voice whispered her name.

Abbie's body screamed with desire for him. She wanted him to take her in his arms and make mad passionate love to her. She wanted to belong to him—forever. But she only stared at the floor while she fought her secret yearnings.

"Yes?" Her toes curled inside her shoes, but she would not raise her head.

"Would you look at me?"

She heard the pleading in his deep voice and couldn't resist him. She looked up into his narrowed dark eyes.

"I want to kiss you."

Abbie's eyes blinked rapidly. She knew he wasn't asking her permission. He was giving her time to turn him down.

"I want to be sure it's not going to scare you." He turned his body towards hers. "After..."

Abbie nodded vigorously. He folded her into a tight embrace and bent his head to kiss her. A tide of passion caught her up and swept her away at the first touch of his lips...a tide that should have transported them both to another world. She pressed into his tantalizing body and gave herself up to the magic of kissing someone she loved. Tom lowered her gently onto the wide couch and lay down beside her. He kissed her hungrily. Abbie wrapped her arms around his neck and held on to him as if her life depended on it. She begged him with her body to make love to her.

The doorbell rang, once at first, and then insistently.

Tom sat up and stared at the door. Abbie, in a sea of embarrassment, straightened quickly and looked around in confusion. She pulled at her clothing and put a hand to her tousled hair. She peered at Tom shyly as he smiled apologetically and rose from the couch.

Abbie reached to grab her mug of now cool chocolate from the coffee table. She wanted to give the appearance of a casual visitor if someone happened to see her. She turned her head to watch Tom.

When he opened the door, the warm lights of the living room illuminated the face of an extraordinarily beautiful woman. Abbie's heart dropped. A sickening feeling came over her. She knew exactly who this was.

Abbie couldn't hear the conversation at the door, but it lasted for a few minutes. Abbie's heart sank when Tom opened the door wider to let the visitor in.

The woman came into the room with a shake of long, dark, silky hair much like Tom's. She quickly slipped out of a red ski jacket and handed it to Tom who carelessly hung the jacket on the coat tree.

"Hello, I'm Debbie," she said in a singsong voice as she approached the couch and held out her hand to Abbie.

Abbie reached up to shake the slender hand. Her eyes flickered back and forth between Debbie and Tom. They were so much alike. It seemed obvious that Debbie was Alaska Native as well. Abbie thought irrelevantly that he had never mentioned that, though why should he have? What business was it of hers?

"Abbie," she introduced herself.

"Do you want anything to drink?" Tom asked Debbie as he stood uncertainly by the front door.

"How about some coffee?" Debbie asked with a smile as she sat down on the opposite couch and scrutinized Abbie appraisingly.

Abbie turned to look at Tom. His face was unsmiling, and he kept his eyes on his ex-wife. He did not see Abbie watching him as he nodded briefly and headed into the kitchen.

"So, I hear you're visiting Alaska. Tom mentioned you at dinner. How do you like it here?" Debbie asked casually.

Abbie studied her rival. Her glistening jet black hair framed an exotic face, long almond-shaped eyes, and full heart-shaped lips sporting bright red glossy lipstick. Tight-fitting dark blue jeans molded over a slender figure, and her red sweater matched the color of her lips. Large silver hoop earrings danced about her cheeks as she turned her head.

Abbie felt plain and frumpy when she looked at the bird of paradise masquerading as a human. She could not compete with this beauty. How could Tom possibly choose her over the bright creature sitting across the room?

"I love Alaska," Abbie said with a forced nonchalance. "I used to live here." Even to her ears, this sounded like a pathetic attempt to belong. But she didn't belong here, she thought futilely. Not like Tom and Debbie did. She was just a tourist...nothing more. Alaska was not her home, and it was never likely to be. She returned her gaze to Debbie who continued to coolly assess her.

"Oh really?" Debbie murmured without interest. "And how did you meet Tom?" she asked with a speculative lift of a well-groomed eyebrow.

Abbie understood. Debbie considered her a rival as well. She wanted Tom back. The words didn't need to be said. That must have been why she contacted him. Abbie had hoped it was something more innocuous, but she now knew Debbie was prepared to reclaim her man.

"On the airplane." Abbie offered no more.

Tom returned to the room. His eyes darted between Debbie on one couch and Abbie on the other. Debbie patted the couch next to her invitingly, but Tom moved over to sit in the easy chair.

"The coffee will be ready in a minute," he said leaning back in the overstuffed chair. He met Abbie's gaze, but she couldn't read his expression. His eyes were veiled, and she felt bereft and alone. She would have jumped up and left with some polite excuse if only she had her own car. As it was, she was trapped here with no way to get back to the hotel. What had just an hour earlier been a rescue had now turned into another miserable nightmare. How could she leave? Did taxis even come out to such a remote location?

"Well, Tom," Debbie said lightly, "Abbie and I were just getting acquainted, but I was hoping to have a few words with you...in private. I don't think we finished our conversation at dinner. You ran out of the restaurant so quickly."

Abbie cringed. Where could she go? Her eyes searched around wildly for a way out.

Tom frowned. "Abbie is staying the night here. She...uh...had a difficult experience in town tonight, and I brought her here for her safety. I'm not sure we'll be able to have a private conversation this evening."

Abbie could have died. Obviously unwanted and in the way, she wracked her brain trying to find a way to salvage the remnants of her pride.

"I don't mean to intrude," she began breathlessly. "Is there a cab I could call? Do they come out here? Or perhaps you could drive me back to town right now, Tom, and come back and...?"

Tom turned a blank face towards her. No lingering sign of the kind man who'd brought her here or the passionate lover who had kissed her only a short while ago remained on his face.

"Taxis don't come out this far. I think you should stay here," he said in a firm, if distant voice. "Debbie and I can step outside if we really need to speak in private."

Debbie's long-lashed eyes flitted between the two of them. A small smile curved her lips.

"Sure, Tom. We can talk outside...later. I'm in no rush. I've got plenty of time."

Abbie's hands curled around her mug. How could she get out of here? She felt so miserable. Tom had become an icy stranger. Debbie no doubt laughed at the foolish female tourist who had probably come all the way to Alaska to find a man.

She made a decision.

"Tom, if you don't mind, I'm exhausted. Could you point the way to the spare bedroom? I think I'm ready to get some sleep."

Tom's frown deepened. Abbie kept her face blank and polite. Out of the corner of her eye, she could see Debbie's smile widen.

Bird of Paradise, my foot! More like a preening peacock! Abbie gritted her teeth.

Tom rose slowly.

"Are you sure?" Inscrutable eyes searched her face. "It's still early."

"Yes, I'm sure. I'm really exhausted. I appreciate you opening your home to me for the evening, and I don't want to be in the way. I'm ready for bed." She rose decisively with a bright smile plastered on her face.

"Good night," she said to Debbie. "It was nice meeting you."

Debbie stood up to shake Abbie's hand. "It was nice meeting you too. I didn't mean to rush you off."

"No, no," Abbie continued her award winning performance. "Like I said, I'm just tired."

"Perhaps I'll see you again in the morning," Debbie added in a low voice that only Abbie could hear as she moved away to follow Tom down the hall.

Abbie's spine stiffened at Debbie's words. *In the morning? Is she staying the night? In Tom's room?* He only had one spare bedroom that she could see. Her stomach knotted, and she pleaded with Tom's broad back. But he did not see her.

He opened the door to a comfortable appearing, albeit sparsely furnished, bedroom. The four poster bed boasted a thick, fluffy white quilt. Plump, clean pillows enticed the head to rest, but Abbie didn't care. She wasn't going to sleep a wink. The master bedroom lay right next door, and she knew she would listen for sounds in the cabin all night long.

"I hope you have everything you need in here," Tom said politely, stepping back to let her in. "Call me if you need anything. You know where the bathroom is. Help yourself to anything in the kitchen."

Abbie stood in the room and nodded mutely, but kept her eyes downcast. He couldn't know how she felt. She wouldn't let him know. His life seemed complicated enough.

"Abbie?" he began tentatively. He reached out a hand to her.

"Yes?" she asked tremulously. She fought to keep

herself from begging him to choose her. Her anxious eyes flew to his face. His eyes softened. He gave her a pleading look.

"Tom, I think the coffee is ready. Do you want a cup?" Debbie called from the living room.

Tom turned his head in the direction of her voice. His face shut down again, leaving it closed, unreadable. He dropped his hand to his side.

"I'll be right there," he called down the hall. He turned to Abbie.

"Goodnight, Abbie. I hope you sleep well."

"Thank you. I will," she said and watched the door shut behind him.

She heard his footsteps recede down the hall, and she reached over to turn off the light in the room. She craved total darkness. A deep, searing sense of shame consumed her. He'd made his choice, and he'd chosen his ex-wife. That seemed clear. *After all, he can just tell Debbie to leave if he doesn't want her here. Can't he?*

Abbie ran a finger over her bruised lips. Why had he kissed her? She could have sworn they were on the verge of making love before Debbie's untimely arrival. She felt dizzy. First, he kissed her, then he said he needed to have dinner with his ex-wife, then another passionate embrace where they come close to making love, and now he made coffee for his ex-wife. What was going on?

How could she have been so foolish...again? First George and now Tom. Was she such a poor judge of men?

In darkness, she made her way to the bed and sat down. The light of the moon filtered through the window curtains, bathing the room in a soft glow. Heightened senses brought the sound of Tom and Debbie's voices near. The indistinguishable words eluded her, but she cringed when she heard an occasional low chuckle from Debbie. Abbie wished she could have been a mouse in a crack in the wall so she could hear their words. She had one small glimmer of hope—as long as they continued to talk, they probably weren't making love.

She took off her shoes and lay down on top of the bed as rigid as a corpse. Through a slit in the curtains, she gazed at the full moon. With bittersweet yearning, she wished she were far away, sitting on top of the moon watching the world. Dangling her feet over the edge, she could study the lights of the planet below and search for Tom's cabin. In her fantasy, he might gaze up at her wistfully before returning to the cabin to turn out his bedroom lights. Debbie's car would be long gone, and Abbie would know that Tom slept alone. She'd watch over him as he slept peacefully.

Abbie continued to hear the voices in the living room. She still couldn't distinguish words, but she heard Debbie's voice grow louder while Tom's voice deepened. *What's going on out there?*

Despite her anxiety, Abbie found her eyelids growing heavy. *I'm not falling asleep, am I? What if...what if I never know? What if I wake and Debbie is still there in the morning, and I never know if they slept together?*

Despite her anxiety, her exhausted eyes closed and she drifted off to sleep.

****

She chased a bull moose that ran from her. She only wanted to pet him, but he continued to crash through the underbrush to escape her. An eagle swooped down, its sharp talons clawing at her face. The exotic bird tried to keep her from catching the moose.

She awoke to hear Debbie's voice in the hallway outside her room.

"I just need to use the bathroom. I'll be right there," Debbie's voice was low, almost a whisper.

Abbie opened her eyes. A sliver of light from the hallway shone under the door. Her heart stopped for a moment and then started pounding in her throat. *I'll be right there?* This wasn't happening. Couldn't they wait until she was gone? Did they have to reconcile tonight...with her still in the house? Why had he kissed her tonight?

"I'll wait," Tom said in his deep voice. His voice came from the hallway as well.

Abbie held her breath and hugged herself tightly. She heard the bathroom door close. Debbie must have gone inside. Footsteps moved down the hallway past her room. The door of the master bedroom creaked as it moved. Debbie came out of the bathroom. Abbie heard Debbie's low voice again as she entered the bedroom next door. The door shut. Abbie could hear their murmured voices. The last thing she heard before she slammed the pillow over her head was the creaking of the bed in the next room. Her silent sobs drowned out all noise as her body writhed with grief. No one should have to suffer this much, she silently screamed. No one should have to lie quietly while the man she adored made love to another woman in the next room. This was straight out of a horror movie.

She pressed the pillow down so hard she couldn't breathe. She hoped against hope she wouldn't hear any more sounds. She couldn't bear to hear them make love. Why hadn't she left? Why hadn't she insisted Tom take her home? Why hadn't she just walked out? So what if she wandered down a dark road into the Alaskan wilderness at night? Anything would be better than this torture.

Abbie's already bruised lip was swollen from biting on it to keep herself from crying out. She turned over on her side to look at the moon, moving the pillow to her other ear. Why couldn't she be sitting on that moon right now, safe, happy, and wise?

Maybe she could leave now. She pushed her watch light and checked the time. It was two in the morning. The sun wouldn't rise for a few hours. She would have to wait until first light and then she would leave. She didn't care how far she was from town. She would make her way back on foot or catch a ride once she reached the highway. Anything was better than facing the lovebirds in the morning.

Exhausted from crying, she closed her aching eyes and drifted off to sleep once again.

Chapter Ten

Abbie opened painful, swollen eyelids. She took the pillow off her head and gazed blearily out the window. The sky was dark gray, but she could see a glimmer of yellow and red light breaking through the evergreen trees. She checked her watch, 7 a.m. Sitting up, she listened for sounds in the room next door.

The cabin was quiet.

She bent to grab her shoes and tiptoed over to the door, pausing to listen intently. She heard nothing. Grateful that the door opened quietly, she peered out into the hall. The cabin remained dark, the door of the master bedroom still shut. She wished she didn't have to use the bathroom, but she did. There seemed to be no way to flush the toilet silently, and she held her breath as the last sounds of running water died away. She cowered in the bathroom, holding her breath, dreading the creak of the door to Tom's room. Nothing.

She wondered where the dogs were. Did they sleep in the master bedroom? Even when he had guests?

Abbie tiptoed out to the living room. Everything looked the same. Three mugs sat on the coffee table.

A wistful desire to see the lake behind the cabin propelled her toward the back door to make her escape. She would never have a chance to see Tom's lake again, and she was determined she would have this memory to take back with her.

As soon as Abbie got back to town, she had every intention of calling the airlines to reschedule her flight for the next available departure. Exhausted, discouraged, and heartbroken, she'd had enough. She wanted to go home, back to her dull life where nothing ever happened, but nothing ever hurt either.

Abbie slipped on her shoes when she reached the back step and tiptoed quietly down the narrow wooden stairs. She followed a well-worn path through luscious and aromatic pine trees to the edge of the small lake. Like an amethyst stone, the lavender light of dawn gleamed on the water. Enthralled by the magnificent view, Abbie envied Tom his small bit of Shangri La. Imagine coming here whenever one was troubled. No breeze moved in the chill morning air, and the calm water perfectly reflected the purple, red, and gold streaks of light in the early morning sky. The scene soothed her jangled nerves. The snow capped mountains in the distance crowned the landscape portrait of the multicolored lake and the surrounding sturdy evergreens. An occasional hungry fish broke the stillness of the water, jumping at some unfortunate insect on the surface.

She sat down on a large boulder at the lake's edge and planned her imminent departure. She'd walk down the road until she got to the main highway. Then she'd catch a ride back into town. Tom had given her wallet back to her, so she had cash to get back to the hotel. She would pack her bags, check out, and take her rental car back to the airport where she would entrench herself until a flight became available.

Afraid the occupants of the cabin would stir and come looking for her, Abbie pushed off the rock to begin the long trek down the road to the main highway. With one last wistful look, she turned away from the lake and walked directly into the path of the two huskies as they padded silently up to her with big grins and wagging tails.

Abbie looked past them and saw Tom walking toward her. He came from a path to the left which seemed to lead around the perimeter of the lake. So...he had not been in the cabin when she rose. Was Debbie still there—in bed?

"Abbie," he said with surprise. "I didn't know you were up. I would have made some hot chocolate if I'd know you were going to wake up so early."

Abbie had desperately hoped to escape before she saw him again. She didn't want to hear about his reconciliation with his wife. She didn't want to hear the words, "Debbie and I are back together." She didn't want to hear anything he might say. Whatever it was, it would hurt.

"Tom! I was just...I was just leaving." She knew he

wasn't going to let her go on foot. She wanted to get away from him before he said anything.

"What?" he asked a frown between his brows. "You weren't planning on walking, were you?"

"Yes," she said as she began to move away. Could she run? Would he chase her? She felt like she'd lost her mind. How could she stop him from saying the words she didn't want to hear? Stick her fingers in her ears and start singing loudly?

"Yes," she repeated in a rush. "I thought I'd walk. I hoped to get away before you woke up."

Her choice of words did not go unnoticed.

"You hoped to *get away*?" he emphasized with a set expression hardening his face. "Have I become an ogre like George that you have to *get away* from me now?" Angry eyes bored into hers. She could have kicked herself for her poor choice of words.

"No, no, I didn't mean it like that," she stammered. "I just hoped to get back to town without disturbing you...that's all," she finished lamely.

"I'll take you back," he said in a cold voice. "You don't need to run off into the wilderness to *get away* from me."

Her heart sickened at his icy tone. She wasn't sure why he was angry with her, and she didn't care. She was just desperate to get away from him. To sit with him for the one-half hour return trip to town would be excruciating.

"I'm fine, Tom. It's not that far back. I really would rather go alone."

She turned again as if to leave, but he caught her arm.

"No," he said roughly. "You're not walking. I'm taking you back. You're being silly."

She looked down at his hand on her arm and shook him off angrily.

"Silly? Silly? Me? I'm not being silly," she started sobbing in exhaustion and frustration. "I'm not being silly."

He stuffed his hands in his pockets. His face softened and he searched her wet and crumpled face.

"Abbie, what's wrong? Talk to me," he pleaded in a deepened voice. The dogs sat patiently by watching the couple.

"Nothing," she said in a muffled tone and blew her nose into a tissue she extracted from her pocket. "Nothing's wrong. I'm tired, and I just want to go home," she mumbled with downcast eyes.

Where was Debbie? What if she walked out of the cabin right now, Abbie wondered with rising hysteria?

Tom moved forward as if to take Abbie in his arms, but she put her hands up to stop him.

"Don't. Don't," she repeated keeping her eyes fixed on the ground.

He backed off with a grim expression on his face.

"Thank you for everything, Tom. I have to go, and I don't want to go with you."

"Abbie, I don't understand. What happened?"

"Nothing happened. I'm just finished, that's all. I'm done. I can't do this anymore," she shook her head in a daze. She turned with finality to walk away, and Tom grabbed her arm once again.

She shook him off again, but this time he refused to let go of her, and he pulled her firmly into his arms. Frustrated, confused, hurt, and angry, she pushed against him with all her might, but he would not let her go. She didn't feel frightened as she had last night when George grabbed her. She knew Tom would never hurt her physically. And she was right. He put a gentle hand over her head and pressed it to his chest. She could hear his heart beating loudly, and she stopped fighting. She leaned against him and soothed herself with the reassuring sound of his heart. Like a wild animal, weakness overtook her as he held her in a firm embrace.

"Please don't leave me, Abbie," he said to the top of her head. She heard the comforting rumble of his voice through his chest, but she wasn't sure what he had actually said. Did he ask her not to leave him? What about Debbie?

She looked up at him through tear-stained eyes as he loosened his hold on her.

"What?" she asked through a fog of confusion.

"Please don't leave me," he repeated as he bent down to take her face in his hands. His eyes were bright as he kissed her wet face hungrily. He kissed her forehead and then her cheeks. His lips traveled over her chin and up to her eyelids. He placed a feather kiss on her nose and found his way home to her mouth. He pulled her to him tightly and took her mouth in his as if he would never let her go.

Abbie responded by wrapping her arms around his neck and holding on to him for all she was worth. Debbie's image disappeared from her mind as she sought only to meld her body with his. They tried desperately to connect through their kiss as they held on to each other.

Abbie was the first to break away, though Tom did not let her out of his arms.

"What about Debbie?"

"She's gone," he said quietly, his eyes glittering as they looked into hers. "She left last night."

Relief flooded over Abbie making her knees weak.

"Are you getting back together with her?" she asked timidly, hoping the truth would be bearable.

He smiled down at Abbie's wet face and put a gentle finger to her swollen lips.

"No. Of course not. I've never had any plans to reconcile with her. I'm in love with you."

Abbie's already shaky knees buckled, and Tom grabbed her tightly as she faltered.

He loves me! Was it possible? Do people fall in love that fast?

Abbie couldn't bear the intensity of his eyes as they searched hers. She buried her face in his chest, the sound of his heart sure and strong.

"Abbie?"

She heard the rumble in his chest.

"Yes?" she mumbled against his jacket.

"Did you hear me?"

Abbie didn't trust herself to speak. She nodded her head up and down.

Tom sighed and enveloped Abbie in a smothering embrace. She responded by wrapping her arms around him and holding on for dear life.

"Why don't you come back inside and I'll heat up some hot chocolate for you?" He set her back from him so he could bend down to study her face. "I'll make breakfast. What do you say?" he coaxed.

Ashamed of her behavior and embarrassed she had let him see her abandoned desire, Abbie found it difficult to meet his eyes. She trusted him with her safety and her life, but she didn't know if she could trust him with her heart. She blinked as she looked up at him. His handsome face gazed at her lovingly. Maybe it was she who couldn't trust her own heart.

"Okay."

Tom took Abbie by the hand and led her back into the house. He removed her coat and hung it by a hook on the back door.

"Why don't you just sit down here and relax?" He led her to a small square pine dining table in the center of the kitchen.

Abbie sat and watched in bemusement as Tom opened cupboards and pulled out pans in preparation for breakfast. The smell of coffee soon permeated the kitchen and he brought a steaming cup of her favorite cocoa over to her. With the delivery, he bent down to kiss the top of her head. She wondered if her heart could take any more. She smiled her thanks, stricken by a shyness that rendered her mute.

While Abbie admired the sensually domestic sight of Tom making breakfast, she wondered if her life was changing. She loved him. He said he loved her. Everything appeared brighter. The cabin seemed warmer. She felt prettier. He looked more handsome than ever.

What would the future hold for them? Would they be together? Would they travel to see each other once or twice a year? How would this relationship work? *Was* there a relationship?

Abbie hesitated to stare at the future too closely. It seemed complicated and discouraging. They lived so far away from one another. She dropped her eyes to the warm mug in her hands. Once before, she had contemplated entering into a relationship with a man who lived in Alaska, but she'd never known the craving to be with George that she felt with Tom. She couldn't bear to leave him now.

Tom set a large plate with an omelet and toast in front of her. The food smelled delicious. Abbie thanked him quietly and wondered how she could possibly eat. Her stomach fluttered with excitement of the first flush of love. Every nerve in her body tingled, ready for what might happen.

Tom sat down across the table from her and dug in heartily.

Abbie picked at her food. It tasted great. He was an excellent cook, but she had no appetite.

"What's wrong? Aren't you hungry?" Tom put down his fork and looked over at her with concern.

"I guess I'm not hungry. I'm sorry," Abbie said with regret. She wanted to eat, but her stomach continued to do somersaults.

He pushed his plate away and took a drink of his coffee.

"Maybe you didn't like the way I made it," he inquired with a broad smile and raised brows.

"Oh no, it's delicious," she reassured him anxiously. "Really, it was. I just...I just can't seem to eat right now."

Tom tilted his head to the side with an unreadable expression. He reached across the table to take her hand. An electric charge shot up her arm. She resisted, but Tom kept a firm grasp. He rubbed the back of her hand with his thumb and gazed at her intently, question in his glittering eyes. She was afraid she knew what the question was, but what was the answer? Would she have to say the words? Could he read her face? Did she even know what she wanted?

Tom must have found his answer because he stood up, came around the table and pulled her up and into his embrace. He bent his head to kiss her lips, gently at first, with tenderness as he explored her mouth. She feared her racing heart might stop from the exquisite sensations his kiss aroused in her. She wrapped her arms around his neck and stood on tiptoe to meld her body into his. Tom groaned and enfolded her more tightly into his embrace. His kiss deepened, insistent and demanding as he asked the question again. Abbie answered with her own mouth returning his kiss hungrily. She moved against him as she begged him with her body to make love to her.

Tom reared his head and searched her face.

"Yes," Abbie breathed. "Oh, please," she begged.

He swung her up in his arms and carried her down

the hall and into the bedroom. By the rosy light of the early Alaskan fall morning, Tom and Abbie at last came together in a fiery explosion of passion and love.

****

Abbie awoke to hear birds singing outside the bedroom window. She found herself lying on Tom's chest, his arm around her shoulder. She rose carefully on one elbow to look down at the man who had given her so much pleasure only a short while ago. His gleaming hair spread across the pillow framing his angular masculine face. She looked down at his full lips and warmed once again as she remembered the sensation of his kisses on her body. Her eyes traveled down his broad and muscular chest to his flat stomach where the bed sheet covered the rest of his strong body. She longed to run her hand down his chest, but avoided waking him up. Once he was awake and alert, she wasn't sure she would have the courage to stare at him to her heart's content as she did now.

Their lovemaking stunned her with its perfection. She gave herself to him without reserve. Abbie trusted him implicitly, and she'd allowed him to give her pleasure without embarrassment. He had been a generous lover. Her body grew warmer still as she remembered their passionate union.

She sighed and laid her head back down on his firm chest. She closed her eyes and listened to the comforting sound of his steady heartbeat as she slept once again.

****

Tom listened to the sound of Abbie's breathing. When it deepened, he opened his eyes and gazed at her face. He'd awakened when Abbie laid her head on his chest, but he decided to let her go back to sleep. He loved the feel of her silky hair on his chest, the softness of her skin as she lay in his arm, and the way her body molded to his in such a perfect fit.

He was glad he'd caught her before she had a chance to run away this morning. Walking and hitchhiking back to town! He didn't even want to think about how furious he would have been if he'd discovered her gone when he returned to the cabin. Furious with himself for bungling the whole thing.

Debbie...she just didn't give up. He'd told her no last

night when they'd met for dinner. No...no reconciliation. Why didn't she understand? Every few years, in between boyfriends, she came back to Alaska asking if he would take her back, and every few years he told her no. It's not like he hadn't thought about it. He'd desperately wanted her to return to him when she'd first left, but she'd been too enthralled with the guy she'd run off with. Tom still didn't know his name, but it didn't matter. Debbie had fallen in love many times since and had moved from man to man in search of something that no one could deliver. It had taken Tom years to forgive himself for not being man enough to keep her.

Debbie's face had taken on a stricken look when he'd told her he was in love with Abbie. He'd seen the look before...many times. Then she tossed her hair, smiled brightly and wished him well. He didn't believe her well wishes, but he had a feeling that she would finally let him go. He hadn't been in love since their marriage, and she'd counted on him being available to her every time she was in between men.

"We're not getting back together, Debbie. I've told you that over and over. Why can't you understand that?" he had asked her in frustration last night.

"Because you still love me, Tom. You always have. We're meant to be together." Debbie clutched the front of his shirt and pulled him to her.

"No," Tom said gently prying her fingers loose. "We aren't meant to be together. You left me a long time ago, Debbie. It's over. My life is different now. I want other things. I'm in love with Abbie"

Tom surprised himself. He hadn't meant to tell Debbie how he felt about Abbie. He'd only just realized it himself, and he hadn't had time to adjust to his emotions. It seemed too private to share with anyone...maybe even with Abbie...certainly not with Debbie.

He liked the sound of it though. *I'm in love with Abbie.*

Debbie pulled away from him as if he were a leper. She looked down at the floor for a moment and then back up into his eyes, a practiced smile on her face.

"Well, well, well. At long last. I wondered when you'd find someone else," she laughed lightly, her eyes glittering with unshed tears. "Abbie," she mused. "I wondered how you felt about her when you mentioned her at dinner. Is she in love with you?"

Tom moved away from her to stand by the front door with his hand on the knob.

"I hope so. I really don't want to discuss her with you, Debbie. I hope you don't mind." He turned the knob. "I think you should probably leave now, okay?"

"Wait, wait a minute," she said breathlessly, her eyes darting around the room. "I need...I need that picture of the two of us in Hawaii. Do you remember? On Waikiki? Could you get it for me?"

Tom's shoulders slumped.

"Oh Debbie, why do you need that?" he sighed. "Just let it go."

She kept the artificial smile on her face, but her eyes continued to glitter.

"I just need to have it, Tom. That's all. I didn't take anything with me when I left, and I've regretted it ever since. Please let me have this one little thing," she pleaded as she moved towards him once again.

"All right," he said in a resigned tone. "It's probably in a box of pictures in my room. I'll go get it."

She'd followed him down the hall. When he'd turned to ask her where she was going, she said she needed to use the bathroom.

"Okay, I'll wait out here in the hall in case Abbie wakes up. She's trying to get some sleep, or at least I hope she is. So, please try to be quiet."

"I will," she whispered as she followed him down the hall.

Tom saw no light under Abbie's door and assumed she was asleep, grateful she wouldn't know how long Debbie had stayed. He planned to explain the reason for Debbie's visit to her in the morning, but he didn't know how to broach the subject. She didn't seem to trust him. She seemed so skittish at times. He grinned at the closed door. But then again, that was one of the things he found so appealing about her.

Certain Abbie was asleep and anxious to see Debbie gone, he went to his room to get the pictures. He shut the door behind him quietly. Debbie could wait in the living room.

He pulled the box of pictures out of his closet and rummaged through them for the pictures of Hawaii. He stared at them, surprised at how detached he felt. They were old memories now, and he didn't mind if she took the whole bunch of pictures with her.

He looked up in surprise as Debbie came into the bedroom. She closed the door behind her.

"I don't want to wake Abbie," she whispered.

He shrugged.

"Here, why don't you take the whole bunch?" he said as he extended the entire packet of pictures toward her.

"Oh, Tom," Debbie said with a crack in her voice. She sat down on the edge of the bed. Tears spilled down her cheeks. She gazed at him with mournful eyes. "Don't you want to keep any of them?"

Tom's chest tightened as he watched her cry. He couldn't bear to make women cry. It made him feel so heartless.

"Okay, Debbie, okay, don't cry. I'll keep a few." He took half the stack and put them back into the box. He bent down and gave her a gentle hug to console her.

Debbie stood up and slipped into his arms, her tears suddenly turned off.

"Tell me that you don't still feel something for me, Tom. Tell me the truth. I know you do," she urged as she pressed against him with her arms wrapped around his neck.

Tom shook his head firmly and pulled her arms away from him.

"No, Debbie, no. Stop this," he said in a dull voice. "Please," he added with finality. He felt bone tired, and he wanted her to leave. He worried about Abbie next door. What if she heard Debbie in his room?

She glared at his fatigued face.

"Oh, fine," she said petulantly as she stepped back. "It seems pretty clear to me that you never really loved me anyway." She stared down at the photos in his hand with disgust. "I don't need those after all. I hated Hawaii, and I hated living there with you."

Tom remembered a time when her words had the power to hurt him, but he felt only a mild distaste when he listened to her now. The pain of loving her was finally gone, leaving him renewed, liberated.

"I know, Debbie, I know." He shook his head gently at her angry face. "I think you'd better go now. Keep in touch and let me know how you're doing, okay?" He opened the door of the bedroom and ushered her down the hall and to the front door.

Debbie turned to him.

"You know, Tom, this Abbie thing isn't going to work out. How can it? What are you guys going to do? Is she going to move up here? Are you going to move down there? Have you given this any thought?" she laughed mirthlessly. "Call me if it doesn't work out."

Tom pulled open the front door and let in the cleansing cool night air.

"Goodbye, Debbie, have a safe drive back to town," he said gently in a voice devoid of emotion.

"You'll be sorry, Tom. I was the best thing you had." She turned and stalked away to her car.

Tom watched to see her get into her car and pull away in a cloud of dust, and then he shut the door on that part of his life forever.

He walked down the hall slowly and paused at Abbie's door. So, he thought, I'm finally in love. He put the palms of his hands flat on the door and pressed his forehead against it, wishing he had the courage to enter the room and take her into his arms. He wanted to make love to her, to feel her body against his and bury his face in her hair. He would lose himself in her kiss.

But Debbie had ruined the moment. He returned to his room, turned out the lights and lay down on his own bed instead. Sleep eluded him as he thought about the woman in the next room and wondered how he could find a way into her heart.

Chapter Eleven

Abbie felt Tom stirring beneath her, and her eyes flew open. She moved away.

"Hey, where are you going?" he asked in a husky voice pulling her back into his arms.

Abbie peeked shyly into his face. His dark eyes shone as he grinned and kissed her forehead.

He lifted her body so her eyes were level with his, and he turned on his side to face her. His warm breath fanned her cheeks, renewing the memory of their passionate kisses.

She lowered her lids to hide her innermost thoughts from his penetrating gaze.

"Good morning," he said in a voice made rough by sleep.

"Good morning," she whispered glancing at him through her lashes.

"Still shy, huh?" he chuckled as he eased her body closer to his.

Abbie smiled. "I can't help it, I'm sorry. This is so *intimate.*"

"I should say so," Tom chuckled languorously. "I should say so," he repeated slowly as he caressed her hair.

Abbie longed to touch his hair with the same tenderness, but something held her back. She closed her eyes again and wondered how she could have made passionate love to him only moments before and yet struggle to touch him spontaneously.

He kissed her forehead once again, and she luxuriated in the sweet sensation of his lips. Her throat ached with the wonder of his touch. Why did she hold back? She could give herself to him with wild abandon. Why then couldn't she reach out to him with all the longing she felt? Why couldn't she show him how much she loved him? What was she afraid of?

"Abbie?"

"Yes?" Her eyes flew to his.

"Is everything all right?" He searched her face intently while he continued to caress her hair.

"Yes," she lied. "No...I mean, yes and no." She couldn't lie into those loving eyes.

"What's wrong?" He rose on one elbow to study her face, allowing his fingers to trace the line of her jaw.

Abbie looked past him to the ceiling.

"I don't know. It sounds silly. I don't know if I can explain." She drew in a deep breath. "I...I want to reach out and caress you like you're touching me, but I can't seem to make myself do it. I'm afraid, I guess," she finished with a sigh.

"Sighing again, huh?" he grinned. "What are you afraid of?"

"I don't know," she answered in frustration. "I don't know."

Tom reached over and took her hand in his. He guided it to his chest, to the spot where his heart beat the strongest.

"Can you feel me?" he asked gently.

"Yes, I can feel your heartbeat. I love the feel of your skin, the sound of your heart. I love to touch you. I just don't know how to make myself reach out to you." Tears blurred her sight, and she blinked them away. What if she was frigid as George had said? Maybe that's why her husband had left her.

"Don't cry, my love. Don't cry," he whispered and bent down to cover her eyelids with soft kisses. "We'll figure it out. It will come. You're just nervous, that's all. So am I," he said and lay down beside her.

She turned to him.

"Really?"

"Oh yeah. You make me very nervous," he chuckled with a sheepish grin. "I feel like I'm back in high school when I'm around you."

Abbie grinned back at him. "Is that a good thing or a bad thing?"

"An awkward thing. I was a mutt in school. None of the girls liked me, no matter what I did to get attention."

"Well, they surely did not know what they were missing," she said appreciatively, instinctively moving closer.

Tom wrapped his arms around her, and she welcomed the delicious warmth of his body against hers. He held her face with one hand while he gazed into her eyes. Finding what he wanted, he leaned in to kiss her with exquisite tenderness, his mouth just brushing her willing lips as he teased her. She pressed against him, begging him to take her again, but he continued to hold back, kissing her deeply and searchingly, waiting, waiting...

"Please, Tom, please," she begged as her head spun to dizzying heights.

"Trust me," he whispered as he made sweet love to her once again.

****

The dogs padded into the bedroom, nudging Tom's hand as it lay on the covers. He woke up and sighed.

"Do they need to go out?" Abbie asked sleepily, awakened by his sigh.

"Yeah. It seems we've been lying in bed all day," he chuckled, reluctantly moved away from her, and stood up.

Abbie relished the chance to see him standing tall and erect without shyness, and she lovingly committed his strong body to memory. What if she never saw him again? What if she returned to Washington, and he never contacted her? What if this was the last time she would be able to see his face...or his body?

He pulled up his jeans and slipped his shirt on before he bent down to kiss her forehead.

"I'll be right back."

"I'm getting up too," Abbie murmured.

She quickly threw her clothes on before he could return. She still felt incredibly shy, though she couldn't understand why. She'd just spent half the day in bed with Tom making the most passionate and sensual love she had ever known. How could she possibly be bashful?

She checked her watch. It was early afternoon. Her flight left at midnight. They hadn't talked about her departure. He hadn't asked. Maybe their lovemaking had been so special because she was leaving. Perhaps he had been saying goodbye to her.

Tom entered the house with the dogs as she came out

of the bathroom.

"How about something to eat?" he asked, a wide grin on his face. "I'm starved."

"Sure," she replied, forcing a smile and followed him to the kitchen. She was leaving tonight. Should she say something to him, remind him? Had he forgotten? Didn't he care?

Abbie's instincts told her that he did care and he had not forgotten. After all, he'd said he loved her. Why then didn't he ask her about her departure? Why didn't he talk about their future together? Was there a future?

Tom searched through the refrigerator and pulled out some luncheon meat and cheese.

"Are sandwiches okay?" he asked as he set plates out on the kitchen counter.

"Sounds great," Abbie said with a false cheeriness.

She sat down at the kitchen table and watched him as he put the sandwiches together. He whistled a quiet tune. The dogs lay in a corner of the kitchen, their frosty blue eyes mirroring the adoration Abbie felt for the cook.

"Here you are," he announced as he set a plate in front of her with a flourish, then sat across from her, and dug into his own food with the same hearty appetite she'd seen at breakfast.

Abbie's stomach knotted, and she found it difficult to eat once again. She wondered how much weight she could lose if she stayed around Tom for long. It seemed as if she was always too nervous or tense to eat.

She bent her head to her food and made a show of eating the delicious sandwich he'd prepared. A multitude of thoughts raced through her mind.

I have to go. Why doesn't he say something? What will happen to us? Why doesn't he say something?

"Tom?" She put her half-eaten sandwich down and looked over at him, hoping the bittersweet yearning she felt didn't show in her eyes.

"Yes, dear?"

"I...my plane leaves at midnight tonight. I'm just reminding you because I have to get back to the hotel to grab my things, check out, and turn the rental car in at the airport."

Please say something. Tell me how or when I'm going

to see you again, she pleaded silently. *Just ask him, you coward, just ask him.* But she couldn't bring herself to do it. She was afraid of the answer.

Tom put his sandwich down, pushed his plate away, and sat back in his chair with a frown between his almond-shaped eyes.

"I know," he sighed. "I know."

He turned to stare out the window towards the trees beyond.

Abbie held her breath waiting for him to say something else, to answer the question she could not bring herself to ask.

To her surprise and distress, he slowly rose and picked up their plates to take over to the sink without looking at her. He began to run water and put soap in.

He was going to wash dishes! Didn't he understand what she needed? Didn't he know she was asking about their future? Abbie knew she wasn't being fair to either one of them. How could he know what she needed to hear? She hadn't asked a specific question. She had simply reminded him that she had to catch her plane. How could he know she was begging him with all her heart to ask her to stay?

Abbie stood up and walked over to the back door. The dogs followed her out and down to the lake.

She looked out over the small lake once again fighting to keep the tears from falling. The leaves blazed with the bright reds and golds of fall. Still no breeze blew, and the calm lake mirrored the surrounding trees.

It was so beautiful here, she thought as her throat burned with the pain of unshed tears. She wondered what it would look like in the summer when the leaves displayed different shades of yellow and green. It seemed likely she would never know. He wasn't going to ask her to stay. She knew with certainty that she wanted to be with him more than anything she had ever wanted before. Of course, she had to return to Washington to give her notice at work, but after that she'd be free to come back to Alaska. But Tom hadn't asked her to return.

She watched the dogs run along the edge of the lake as they futilely attempted to chase the ducks that calmly glided calmly out of harm's way into the middle of the lake.

Abbie heard footsteps approach. Tom put his arm around her shoulder as he came to stand beside her. She glanced at him, but he seemed lost in contemplation of the lake. With a deep sigh, she returned her gaze back to the water as well.

She stood in the place she must have always dreamed of—in the arms of a kind and gentle man, a generous lover, and an intelligent companion. Tom epitomized everything she wanted in a man. He was indeed too good to be true.

"It's beautiful here," she said with a catch in her voice.

"Yes, it is, isn't it? I'm glad you like it," he said apparently unaware of the grief in her voice. He pulled her closer and kissed the top of her head. "It's nice to share it with someone."

Abbie's paused and she held her breath. Was he going to ask her? Was he going to ask her to stay? *Please, please.*

Silence.

Abbie wondered desperately if there was anything she could say that would lead to a discussion of their future. *Gee, Tom, I'm going to go back to Seattle, quit my job, and move up here to live with you?* No, she couldn't just blurt that out—especially—without an invitation. How about *Gee, Tom, would you ask me to come up here and live with you?* Not likely. Or the more mature and clinical *Gee, Tom, let's talk about our future.* Abbie couldn't imagine saying any of those things aloud. It had to come from Tom. And he wasn't asking.

"Well, are you about ready to head back into town? I know you want to have plenty of time to do everything you need to before your flight leaves." Tom gave her another quick hug as he whistled for the dogs and turned toward the house.

"Yes, I'm ready." Abbie slowly followed his retreating back to the house.

****

"Cassie?"

"Abbie! It's about time you called. Well, what's going on? How is it going? Did you patch things up with Tom?"

Abbie leaned back against the headboard of her bed and stared at her packed suitcases waiting by the door.

"Yes and no," she told her best friend with a catch in her throat. She had promised herself she wouldn't cry.

"Uh oh, what's wrong?"

"I don't know where to start," Abbie said with a ragged sigh.

"Well, how about at the beginning? The last time we spoke, I encouraged you to talk to Tom and tell him about your reasons for going up to Alaska. Did you tell him?"

"Yes, I told him...eventually."

"And?" Cassie prompted.

"It seems so much has happened since then. We slept together." Abbie dropped the bombshell, too weary to explain gracefully.

"Abbie! Is that all you're going to tell me? How did that come about? Is this good news? It sounds great to me. Well?" Cassie asked impatiently. "Tell me." Abbie thought about the past week and wondered why she didn't bubble over with excitement to tell Cassie everything. She had come to Alaska expecting nothing. She'd met the most handsome, kind, and loving man, and he said he loved her. He had made love to her in the most sensuous and passionate encounter of her life. And she was miserable. What was wrong with her?

With great effort, Abbie filled Cassie in on the details since she'd last spoken to her.

"So then he drove me back to the hotel and dropped me off. I've packed my bags, and I have to leave in a bit to go to the airport."

"Well, what did he say when he dropped you off? Is he going to meet you at the airport to say goodbye? Did he say when he plans to see you next? Is he going to call? Is he coming down here to visit you? I can't wait to meet him. Did he say *anything*?"

Every one of Cassie's questions dug deeper into Abbie's heart. She'd asked herself the same questions on the ride back to town. Tom had held her hand on the way, occasionally giving her a warm smile. He'd made idle conversation about the scenery, but he'd failed to speak of any possible future together.

"No, not really. He kissed me and gave me one of his

great bear hugs. I felt loved. And then he said he'd call me and drove away."

"Are you kidding? That's all?" Cassie squeaked.

The disbelief in Cassie's voice echoed her own depressed thoughts.

"Did you ask him when you would see him again?" Cassie said on a quieter note. "Did *you* say anything to him, Abbie?"

"No. I didn't. I didn't know what to say. He's lived alone for so long. Maybe he's one of those men who don't need to be in a relationship. Maybe he's happy on his own."

"You said he told you he's in love with you. Do you believe him, Abbie?" Cassie asked gently.

Abbie thought for a moment. She saw Tom's face again in her mind—his smile, the passion in his eyes, the tenderness when he had looked at her this morning.

"Yes, I do. I do think he loves me. So, I don't understand why he doesn't say anything about our future together."

Abbie had no tears left. She had cried and cried when she'd returned to her room a short while ago.

"I'd be ready to move up here tomorrow if only he would ask. I think he's the man I've been waiting for all my life," she continued in a small voice.

"Oh Abbie," Cassie said with a catch in her voice. "I'm so sorry."

Silence filled the line for a short period.

"I need to send Sanjay up there to talk some man sense into Tom," Cassie continued with a small laugh.

Abbie smiled. "I'm smiling. You can't see it and I can't laugh, but I'm smiling. Thanks, Cassie, that sounds like a great idea."

Cassie chuckled.

"What are you going to do?"

"I don't think there is anything to do. In my wildest imagination, I've dreamed of asking him if I could come live with him or if he'd come live with me or even if we're going to see each other two or three times a year, but I can't imagine actually saying those things. What if he said no?"

"Why would he, Abbie? He said he loves you."

"Then why hasn't he said something? Why did he just drop me off at the hotel?"

"I don't know," Cassie said in a mournful tone.

"Me either," Abbie sighed.

Cassie's tone brightened. "Well, listen. You come home, and we'll sit down and brainstorm this thing together. There has to be a way. We'll find the right thing for you to say. Who knows? Maybe after you've been gone for a month or two, he'll find he misses you so much, he'll come to visit you."

Abbie smiled. Cassie and her optimism!

"Not everyone can find what you and Sanjay have, Cassie. It's not all that common, you know."

"It sounds like you found your man, Abbie. Now, it's just a matter of logistics."

"And trust," added Abbie.

"What do you mean?"

"I always imagined that when I fell in love again, everything would be perfect. My life would be magical. I would never be alone again. But even when we were wrapped in each other's arms, I couldn't reach out to touch him. I couldn't initiate contact. You know...touch his face, his lips, though I wanted to so badly. I wait for him to touch me. Does that make sense?"

Cassie didn't answer right away.

"Cassie?"

"I'm thinking," Cassie said. "I'm thinking. I'm trying to put myself in your place."

"Oh please do, and give me yours," Abbie chuckled.

"Okay, I've thought," announced Cassie with a flourish, "and this is what I've come up with. I think perhaps you can't reach out to him because you don't trust him not to disappear from your life. And since neither one of you has spoken of a future together, you have no guarantee you will ever see him again. Soooo....I think you're holding back, physically and emotionally. What do you think?"

Abbie sighed. "I think you might be right, Cassie. I knew you'd have the answer. I just couldn't figure it out, but it makes sense now that I hear you say it. I suppose it's the same reason I can't, or won't, ask him when or how I'm going to see him again. It's strange, isn't it? I love him, he loves me, but we're not together. What's keeping us apart?"

She knew the answer even as Cassie repeated it.

"Trust, just like you said, Abbie. Trust."

"How do I learn to trust?"

Cassie paused. "Time...time, and the faithful love of a dependable man."

Abbie cleared her throat. Her chest tightened painfully.

"Time...and a faithful man," she echoed.

The image of Tom's face swam before her, the memory of his gentle touch, the safety of his arms, the love in his eyes.

She sighed. "Okay, I'll give it time."

"Good girl!"

Abbie forced herself off the bed. "Well, dear, I have to get going, so I'll talk to you tomorrow, okay? Thanks for the advice. I needed it."

"All right, Abbie. I'll talk to you in the morning. Take care and have a safe flight home. I hope..." Cassie paused. "I'm hoping for the best," she finished quietly.

"Thanks, Cassie. Bye."

Abbie dragged her bags downstairs and checked out at the front desk. As she got into her rental car, she thought wryly that she could have saved herself some money by never renting it at all. If only she had known she would meet Tom on the airplane, she thought wistfully.

She took her time driving to the airport, savoring the late evening light of the Alaskan fall. She rolled down her window and inhaled the cool evening air. No evidence of frost tickled her nose. Winter approached, and the city would soon be blanketed in a quiet layer of snow. Abbie smiled, remembering the perpetual twilight which darkened the sky for over eighteen hours of the day. The lack of bright light never depressed her as it had others. Keeping up with her children's activities had probably been responsible for averting the sadness which now threatened to paralyze her.

In a fog of depression, she returned the car to the rental agency and wandered into the airport, dragging her wheeled bag behind her. As she neared the place that would take her away from Alaska—from Tom—even breathing seemed like too much effort. All she really wanted to do was sit down on the pavement in front of the airport and cry. She hated to leave, but she couldn't stay. Tom's unwillingness or inability to discuss their future together was an answer in itself. Whatever his reasons for not making plans to see her again, he obviously wasn't so enthralled with her that he begged her to stay.

She checked her bag and passed through security to meander down to her boarding gate. With a listless gaze, she surveyed the other passengers at her boarding gate...remembering the silent question she'd pondered only a few days ago. *What kind of idiot takes an 8 p.m. flight to Anchorage, Alaska, in September anyway?*

Well, what kind of idiot takes a midnight flight out of Alaska in September anyway? She dropped into one of the seats in the waiting lounge and studied her fellow travelers. Were they leaving Alaska forever? Were they simply traveling *outside* for a bit, only to return to loved ones? Was anyone else heartbroken?

She sat in a stupor, unwilling to read her paperback, unable to envision her life beyond today.

The gate agent announced boarding for the flight, and she dragged herself up to stand in line. A line she didn't want to be in.

Only a few passengers boarded the plane as one would expect of a midnight flight. The emptiness and loneliness of the boarding process suited Abbie's mood. She *was* empty and lonely. The last thing she needed was a plane full of cheery, happy travelers off to new and exotic locations. She thanked the stars she wasn't on a morning flight to Hawaii.

Pleased to see her seat assignment at the rear of the plane once again, she had the row to herself. A surge of pain cut across her chest as she looked over at the empty window seat. She could still see the profile of Tom's handsome face as he had looked out the window on the flight to Alaska. She gritted her teeth and moved over to the window seat. She was *not* going to see his face in the seat every time she looked over...or worse yet...see the empty seat. She'd sit in the seat herself and hope no one came to take the aisle seat. But it didn't matter, she thought fatalistically as she laid her head against the cool pane of the window and stared at the darkened tarmac. It didn't matter whether anyone sat next to her or not. She'd sleep to pass the time.

"Ladies and gentlemen, could I have your attention please?" The flight attendant stood at the front and gave the safety instructions. Abbie glanced at her and looked away. She didn't really care about safety on the way back home. Why should she?

She pressed her eyes tightly shut, willing sleep to come. *Please let me sleep through the worst of this pain. Please.*

He hadn't come to the airport to see her off. He hadn't come. Why?

A jolt startled Abbie as the plane pushed away from the terminal. She wanted to scream. *Wait, please wait, I don't want to go. Wait, I'm leaving someone behind.*

They rumbled slowly along the tarmac with an inescapable forward motion. She opened her eyes to take a last look at the airport. The lights burned bright in the darkness. She put her hand up to the window and pretended to wave at someone in the airport, someone she was leaving behind. *Goodbye.*

The plane taxied to the beginning of the departure runway, and the engines roared. She had always enjoyed that moment when the engines revved up. Such power, such a thrill. Soon, the plane would tear down the runway, heave itself up into the sky, and take her off on a new adventure.

But that was then. Now, her insides cramped as she silently pleaded, *please don't take me away. Please leave me here. I've lost something. I've lost someone, and I have to find him*. She felt as desperate as a mother dog whose puppies have been taken away.

But the plane did lift off, the wheels locked, and hot tears rolled down her face. He hadn't come to the airport to say goodbye. Would she ever see him again? How? When?

Abbie looked down to see the bowl of Anchorage lit up once again against the blackness of the night. She didn't know if she would ever see it again. Her head pounded and her jaw ached from tension.

She rested her forehead against the cool window and closed her eyes again, willing sleep. Time and sleep were all that would help with the pain. *Tom...*

Exhausted from the emotions of the last week, her eyelids drooped, and she fell into merciful sleep.

Chapter Twelve

"Excuse me, I think you have my seat." Through the fog of murky sleep, Abbie heard a familiar voice.

Her eyes flew open and she stared up at the tall man towering over the entrance to her row.

Tom!

"Tom! Where...how...what are you doing here?" Abbie tried to jump up, but hit her head on the overhead compartment. "Ouch!"

He chuckled as he reached over to pull her out of the seat and into the aisle. He brought her to him in a crushing embrace and bent his head to kiss her deeply. She wrapped her arms around his neck and clung to him, ignoring the stares of the other passengers and the amused smiles of the flight attendants.

They came up for air to hear the flight attendant saying, "Ladies and gentlemen, due to some turbulence, the captain has turned the seatbelt light back on. Please return to your seats." It wasn't a question.

Abbie returned to her seat, and Tom slid into the seat next to her.

She stared at him in wonder.

"You said you'd call," she said foolishly.

He grinned broadly at her. "I guess you could say this is a call."

"Why didn't you tell me you were flying out tonight? Where..." Abbie still couldn't ask the question.

"I didn't know if I could get on the plane until a few hours ago. I had to get back to the cabin and make arrangements for my neighbor to take care of the dogs." Tom smiled at her tenderly. "I would have come to sit with you right away, but they made me take my assigned seat during takeoff. I couldn't switch until after we'd taken off and leveled out."

"Why?" she asked simply.

"Why wouldn't they let me switch seats?" he teased.

"No, silly. You know what I'm asking. Why?" she repeated with a loving smile.

"I'm coming to help you pack."

"Pack?" she asked in a squeak. Was it possible? Did miracles really happen?

"Yes, pack. I figure you'll want to give two weeks' notice, right? So, I hope I can stay with you for the two weeks. I'll pack while you work. How does that sound?"

Abbie began to understand that her dreams might just be coming true.

"It sounds great. Where am I going?"

"Why, back to Alaska with me, of course," he responded as if the answer had been perfectly clear.

"I am?" she played along.

"Yes, of course. Was there ever any doubt?" He let go of one of the deep sensuous chuckles she loved.

"Yes, as a matter of fact, there were plenty of doubts," she teased, but her wide eyes betrayed her fears.

"Abbie, I love you," Tom said looking into her troubled eyes. He took her hand and brought it to his lips with a tender kiss. "I can't live without you. I don't want to live without you. Please come back to Alaska to live with me. I need you."

He took Abbie's face in both of his hands and kissed her hungrily. Against her lips, Abbie could feel him whisper the words, "I love you."

Abbie kissed him back with all the love burning in her heart, wishing she could throw off the seatbelts that separated them. She wanted to lay with him as she had that morning, his skin warm against hers. In a few hours, she thought, when they reached her home, they would be in each other's arms again. For now, she must be satisfied with the feel of his hands and his lips on her face.

"I love you too, Tom. I can't believe I've finally found you."

He lifted his head and looked deeply into her eyes.

"I'm glad you finally found me, too." His voice was husky with feeling. "I've been lost for a long time."

He bent his head to hers once again and whispered against her lips, "I'm going to marry you...if you'll have me."

Abbie pulled away to look into dark eyes naked with

emotion...pleading, uncertain.

She reached up with a hand and touched his silken hair as it grew from the widow's peak at his forehead. She let her hand travel down the side of his beloved face, caressing his high cheekbones and his firm jaw. He rubbed his face against her hand. Her fingers made their way to his full lips where he kissed their tips. She felt free at last to touch him. She was going to be his. He was going to be hers. She didn't have to hold back anymore. She trusted him. He wasn't going to leave her.

This time, it was Abbie who reached up to kiss his mouth tenderly, savoring his lips as he responded eagerly to her touch.

"Yes, my love, I'll have you. Thank you for bringing me home at last."

As the mighty plane flew into the night, Abbie knew her life was taking flight as well, and she saw the future bright with hope.

And she sighed.

A word about the author...

Bess McBride began her first fiction writing attempt when she was 14. She shut herself up in her bedroom one summer while obsessively working on a time travel/pirate novel set in the beloved Caribbean of her youth. Unfortunately, she wasn't able to hammer it out on a manual typewriter (oh yeah, she's that old) before it was time to go back to school. The draft of that novel has long since disappeared, but the story is still simmering within her, and she will get it written one day soon.

Bess was born in Aruba to American parents and lived in Venezuela until her family returned to the United States when she was 12. She couldn't fight the global travel bug within her and joined the U.S. Air Force at 18 to "see the world." After 21 wonderful and fulfilling years traveling the world and gaining one beautiful daughter, she pursued her dream of finally getting a college education. Armed and overeducated, the gypsy in her has taken over once again, and she is now embarking on a full-time journey in a recreational vehicle as she continues to look for new adventures and place settings for her writing. The Wild Rose Press has helped her fulfill a lifelong dream of writing romances.

Contact Bess at BessMcBride@thewildrosepresss.com

Visit Bess' website at www.bessmcbride.com

Printed in the United States
203746BV00003B/1-21/P

9 781601 541772